White Hunter Grey Heart

White Hunter Grey Heart

Lucas Scott Mark

Copyright © 2023 by Lucas Scott Mark.

Library of Congress Control Number:		2023901346
ISBN:	Hardcover	978-1-6698-6406-6
	Softcover	978-1-6698-6405-9
	eBook	978-1-6698-6404-2

All rights reserved. No part of this book may be reproduced or transmitted in any form or by any means, electronic or mechanical, including photocopying, recording, or by any information storage and retrieval system, without permission in writing from the copyright owner.

This is a work of fiction. Names, characters, places and incidents either are the product of the author's imagination or are used fictitiously, and any resemblance to any actual persons, living or dead, events, or locales is entirely coincidental.

Any people depicted in stock imagery provided by Getty Images are models, and such images are being used for illustrative purposes only.
Certain stock imagery © Getty Images.

Print information available on the last page.

Rev. date: 01/23/2023

To order additional copies of this book, contact:
Xlibris
844-714-8691
www.Xlibris.com
Orders@Xlibris.com
850586

I, Hammurabi, should rule over the black-headed people like Shamash, and enlighten the land, to further the well-being of mankind.
Code of Hammurabi, circa 1727-1680 B.C

And the one idea is, how we are going to exterminate white people because that in my estimation is the only conclusion I have come to. We have to exterminate white people off the face of the planet to solve this problem ⋯ The problem on the planet is white people.
Dr. Kamau Kambon, Howard University School of Law, 2005

Q: What kind of world do you want to leave to your children? **A:** A world in which there aren't any white people⋯
Leonard Jeffries, chairman of the African-American Studies
Department of the City College of New York, 1995

White people are scared, because minorities are taking over. And they are absolutely right. When the shit turns around, we are going to treat you exactly like you've treated us: like shit.
Paul Mooney, Comedian, 1993

The white race is the cancer of human history.
Susan Sontag, white intellectual, 2005

After looking at all the evidence there is only one conclusion: white people are devils I believe that we must secure our freedom and independence from these devils by any means necessary, including violence ⋯ To protect ourselves we should bear arms immediately and form a militia ⋯ So black people, let us unite, organize and execute.
Chino Wilson, Penn State Editorial, 1992

What we need is the destruction of whiteness, which is the source of human misery in the world.
Rev. James Cone, 1999

Recently a shirt with the wording, "It is not illegal to be white...yet," hit the online stores. This is a symbol of the unsaid cultural transformation the U.S. is going toward. A civilization where it is illegal to be white.
Frank Palmer, radio host, KARP, 2012

Contents

I	The Hunt	1
II	The Temple	15
III	The Anointed	61
IV	The Butterfly	75
V	The Debate	89
VI	The Truth	137
VII	The Prophecy	173
VIII	The Cleansing	241

1

The Hunt

1

A sea of leafless gnarled black trees stretches out and grovels beneath an orange sky. Solitude rules in the darkened and stunted trees, no sign of life, man or animal. A once well traveled path, and even longer ago a concrete road, is now desolate. The summer wind keeping the dilapidated branches mobile is the only sound, until a body falls through brush and lands on the rocky ground.

It is a man. He is barely dressed, barbaric, with wild long gray hair, beard, and pale white skin. The man's face is in agonizing distress as he quickly looks around. His eyes fall to examine his arm, caked with fresh blood. He hears something in the distance, jostles his painful and aged body to his feet, and descends a hill into the forest brush.

For a second all is still again, a small puddle of blood and some rustled forest greenery is the only evidence the man was there. But the same brush the man fell through shakes, and a giant silhouette of a man steps through. He spots the blood on the ground, his dark massive figure kneels for a moment to study it before rising and going on. White letters "T-E-E-C-H-E-R" gleam from the man's back through the darkness as he stalks away.

It is Teecher's purpose: To hunt. His life, his joy, his soul. For him, there is nothing greater than the thrill of the hunt, the pulsing blood and adrenaline through his body, utilizing the many deadly tools during the sacred duty, and taking the kill. Like Death himself, Teecher will tread on the carcass of history, controlling the events before him, planning destruction, and making sure the Hunt plays out just as he intends. And it is sacred duty to teach others to do the same.

Teecher's huge muscles bulge as he speaks into his headset radio, "Pay attention Pupil 311, as this is your final lesson."

Down the hill the barbaric-looking white man rests on a tree for a second and listens carefully. A red dot appears on his head. Although unaware a laser has found him, he begins running again.

The man reaches a clearing and realizes he is at the top of a steep hill. He looks back for only a second before going down. He steadies himself for a few feet, but his animal skin boot gets snagged on a branch in the hillside where he falls and rolls down the hill. The man manages to miss two huge boulders in the hillside as he tumbles down, but lands into another large rock at the bottom. He peers at his new wounds only for a second before rising and quickly hobbling away.

Teecher emanates from over the hill, the moon finally illuminating him. Compared to the man he is hunting, he is a giant. His Hunter's uniform is pitch black. His military ranks and medals upon his chest shine under the moonlight, a projection of his numerous feats during many years of active duty. Teecher's dread locks hang from underneath his black helmet, a shield covers his dark brown face.

Not far away, the barbarian hides in a small cavern in the mountain side. He holds his bleeding arm and waits, listening, and staying silent. His eyes widen as he hears a rustling sound above him. Suddenly, a mechanical crane-like hand plummets through the ceiling of the cavern, the metal fingers grab the man's head and pull him up through the soil to above ground.

"You see the how the claw is versatile in its use?" Teecher asks into his headset as he raises the barbarian high above him.

His arm has metamorphosed into a gigantic robotic appendage. The metal phalanges dig into the man's shoulders and neck. He dangles there, bleeding, trapped, screaming in some unfamiliar tongue.

The orange sky seems to burn behind Teecher as he peers up at his prey. Surprisingly, he drops the barbarian down, letting him free. The barbarian can barely stand. He doesn't run as if giving up. Blood gushes from where the robotic arm tore his flesh, every other inch of his pale body spews sweat. He is spent from both his wounds and his run under the scorching sun.

"Last exercise," Teecher radios. Then he puts his hand out to the side with palm up to signal him to go, that he is free.

The barbarian is frozen, not understanding.

The Hunter motions again for him to go and this time he either understands or decides to make a go for it. He glances in both directions before darting downhill and descending further down the mountain side.

Teecher speaks into his radio again, "Now we will utilize the spear."

Teecher casually strides to the hill's crest and watches the man flee momentarily before revealing a silver baton.

"Remember," he teaches, "It's all in the wrist." He whips the weapon toward the barbarian and a chained spear soars from the baton and spirals like a striking snake into the barbarians back with a piercing thud.

The man's pale white body freezes like a caught fish.

Teecher violently pulls the chain toward him, causing the barbarian's body to fly backward and land on the ground in front of his feet. Without hesitation the Hunter draws a sword from his back and chops the barbarian's head off. Teecher turns away from his triumph, sheathes his sword, and activates his radio once again, "Now do you see my pupil what your training has readied you for?"

In the brush beyond the bloody scene the pupil appears, a very young man dressed similarly to Teecher, except chest and shoulders bare of any medals. He stands frozen, as if mesmerized by the barbarian's body.

Teecher glares at the young man. "Speak up Pupil 311! Do you not see the power you now wield?"

The pupil seems confused at first. Finally, he speaks, "I understand what the powers can do."

Teecher replaces his sword behind his back. "Very good," his tone now calm. "You are at the end of your training. There is only the ceremonial Graduation at the Temple and then of course first blood to sanctify you. You are ready to begin your life as a White Hunter."

2

"What is a White Hunter?" The ageless old Hunter called Lecturer asks a small class of young Pupils, his white beard and willowy long and unbraided hair sways back and forth as he speaks.

He eyes the Pupils one by one.

The unit of Pupils does not dare to speak up without knowing what their teacher wants to hear.

The old Lecturer doesn't let up. "After your years of training, disparate they may be due to most of your age differences, each of you should have an answer." He looks to Pupil 315, a sturdy 15-year old, fearless and somehow angst ridden, waiting for his chance to show everyone, including himself, what he is capable.

"It is power," the boy answers through his teeth.

The old man looks as if he knew it was the answer he'd get. He shakes his head no and turns to Pupil 316 and 317, 12-year old twin boys as opposite as one will ever find. "Pupil 316, what is your answer?"

"I believe there are many facets to that answer," Pupil 316 begins to give his ever complicated answers. "For instance-"

Lecturer raises his hand to stop Pupil 316 from talking. "I need a short answer, one or two words please."

Pupil 316 looks as if he has been asked the impossible. He begins to think. "Well-"

"Yes?" Lecturer asks.

"I guess I would say one facet is slightly more important than the rest," Pupil 316 answers finally, "and that is training."

The old Lecturer shakes his head again.

Pupil 317 giggles to himself regarding his brother's wrong answer.

Lecturer asks, "And how about you, oh brother 317?"

Pupil 317's giggle turns into a deer in the headlights. "What?"

"What is a White Hunter?"

Pupil 317 is at a loss. He shrugs. "It is us, I mean you guys, you know," he thinks of something and slowly blurts out, "Those that hunt white people?"

The old man shakes his head. "No." He continues to look at Pupil 317. "No," he says again.

Pupil 317 is confused.

Lecturer goes on to the last student, Pupil 318, a 5-year old who has not been away from his family very long. "I realize you are still new here Pupil 318, but what do you think a White Hunter is?"

The little boy scratches his head, thinks about his birth name and how they keep calling him Pupil 318, then remembers. "They are like cowboys," he answers in a tiny voice, "you know, like the guys that save people."

The old Lecturer gives a slight smile radiating pity. "Good answer." He turns to the whole class once again. "But, wrong as well."

All the Pupils are disappointed.

Lecturer marches to the giant digital black board. "All of your answers were in fact good."

The Pupils cheer up, some look at each other with smiles and nods.

"Yet," Lecturer raises his finger to get the attention of every Pupil, "The correct answer is that a White Hunter is an employee of Godallah. It is a sacred duty." He begins to pace as he lectures. "Now I know you have no idea, any of you, what an employee is. Citizens' food is grown and harvested by auto systems. Robots create our beautiful products like NeezeCola. So no one has jobs or a set duty or duties in the Empire. No one except us. Our duty makes us employees."

The Pupils soak in the information.

"As employee of Godallah and the Empire, your sacred duty is to make sure evil never creeps back into our world." The old man touches a panel on his podium. The digital blackboard lights up with a picture of a white devil.

"This," the old Lecturer states, "is the enemy."

3

The one stop Empire high-speed monorail train halts to a stop at Atlanta station.

"Norlins to Atlanta. 1pm," the mechanical conductor voice announces over the loudspeaker.

"Wake up Monique," Crystal, a light-skinned woman somewhere in her thirties, gives one of her best friends Monique a shove.

"What?" Monique asks, barely awake. She is a darker, smaller woman around the same age wearing a short party dress. She starts to stretch her body from being in the sitting position while sleeping.

Crystal is already standing, her baggage in hand, wearing a similar style dress. "We gotta go now. Those two are at it again."

Monique rubs her eyes. "Who? Cicily and her new friend?"

"Her boyfriend, Monique, now quit your constant attitude and let's go," Crystal tells her as she pulls Monique's bags out from the overhead storage.

"She just met this guy a few days ago," Monique grabs her bags from Crystal. "And if you do the math regarding her usual length in relationships, I'd say it is about up."

"Maybe that is the point then," Crystal replies. "We don't know this guy well."

"I guess you have a point there," Monique says with a yawn. The two turn toward the train door.

Suddenly, Cicily storms into the train cabin. "I cannot believe this guy!"

"Seems like all guys," Monique says dryly.

"Shut up Monique," Crystal orders before looking at Cicily. "Are you OK Cil? Where is he?"

Cicily stands with her hands on her hips shaking her head. She has a party dress on as well, even shorter than the other's. Although similar in figure, she is not as attractive as her two friends. "She's right you know. My life seems to be some indecent ignorant hunt. Day after day searching for a man, a baby's daddy, in all the wrong places."

"Just have fun girl," Monique pleas. "I mean you do anyway. So have fun having fun. If the man you are with right now feels insecure, then forget him. Life is all about having fun. It is the Empire motto."

Crystal steps in front of Monique. "Are we still going to watch your brother's graduation at the Public Theater? It has already begun."

Cicily seems to snap out of it. "Yes, of course. That is why we came back today, isn't it?"

4

Pupil 311 checks his digital watch before entering the lecture hall.

"They are demons, pure evil," Lecturer goes on. He spots Pupil 311 and nods to him before going on. "Now we may be lucky that the whites have been eliminated in the Empire, yet our sacred duty will never end. That is why we keep an elite force of White Hunters, a small force it may be, to police the land in case of their return."

The young Pupils are entranced with the lecture.

Pupil 311 smiles slightly as he remembers his days of lecture. A bell rings.

"It is time for one-on-one pairing with your chosen big brother," the old Lecturer announces.

The Pupils jump up from their class spots and run toward the door.

Pupil 315 sees Pupil 311 in the doorway. "311!" he exclaims.

"Hello," Pupil 311 says. "I will meet you in the hall for our time."

Pupil 315 nods with a bow and exits the lecture hall.

"Congratulations 311," the old lecturing Hunter approaches Pupil 311 and gives him a couple hard pats on the shoulder.

"Thank you, sir." Pupil 311 looks around the lecture hall.

"Miss listening to me babble on, do ya?" Lecturer laughs.

"I kind of do actually."

Pupil 311 looks up at the white man's face. It was the same picture they used when he was going through lectures. The white man resembled the one Teecher killed, but with no facial hair. And for the first time Pupil 311 realizes the picture was doctored with evil eyebrows, weird lips, red eyes, and horns. The white man in the forest showed no signs of any of these traits, no demonic physical signs at all.

"The horns and stuff," Pupil 311 blurts as he points up at the picture.

Lecturer looks back. "The additions?"

"Yes," Pupil 311 answers.

"Just something to stoke the fire we are creating here," the old Lecturer smiles almost evilly at Pupil 311. "Perhaps to entertain a bit as well."

There is an awkward silence, both men looking at each other. "OK," Pupil 311 says finally, "315 is waiting for me."

Lecturer nods. "I will see you at the Temple." He saunters back to his podium. "Congratulations again," he speaks without looking back.

Pupil 311 exits the lecture room to find Pupil 315 practicing fighting forms in the hall. He watches the young boy twist and turn, punch, kick, in his memorized sequence of moves.

"Very good 315," Pupil 311 compliments him.

The young Pupil stops his forms, bows. "Congratulations," he states robotically, "On becoming a Hunter."

Pupil 311 smiles. "Your almost there as well. But thank you."

Pupil 315 nods, keeping his posture standing straight up.

Pupil 311 studies the teen pupil. He is tall for his age, maybe close to six foot, just a solid young man extremely full of life and physical vigor. And this vigor often gives way to anger and angst. And that is exactly what the Academy wants.

"What are we to do today, sir?" Pupil 315 asks.

Pupil 311 had actually forgot all about the day's lesson. He always had a lesson plan for his little brothers. But, the incident with Teecher seemed to have put him in a state of shock.

Pupil 311 thinks quickly before saying, "I thought maybe we could counsel today."

Pupil 315 doesn't seem to be too fond of the idea. But, due to the emphasis in respect and self-discipline during his lifetime of training, he confers. "Yes, sir."

"Let's go to the inner courtyard," Pupil 311 proposes.

Pupil 315 nods and follows Pupil 311 down the hallway to a glass door near the end. The glass automatically slides open as they approach, the orange beams of the sun instantly radiate into the hall. The two step into the inner courtyard and the glass doors close behind them.

Pupil 311 finds the only shaded table and the two sit down on their stone benches. There is a moment of awkward silence. No sounds of birds, or bugs, just the wind whipping over the Academy roof and down into the inner courtyard.

"Man, it is hot," Pupil 315 complains, sweat already pouring from his dark brow. "Why did the Academy even make this inner courtyard space? And every table is under scorching sun!"

Pupil 311 looks down at him. "Haven't you been practicing more outdoor training?"

Pupil 315's eyes shift away. "Yes, I've tried."

Pupil 311 shakes his head. "It's imperative as you get closer to your graduation. The weather outside is brutal. Even citizens wear hats, cool clothes, and some even braid their hair to shade themselves from the sun. You've spent most of your time inside since you came here at 5-years old. You need to get your body adjusted and able to bear vigorous action in this heat."

Pupil 315 looks back at Pupil 311, nods at first, but then scowls. "I was thinking about that. If there are no whites left, then who will I be chasing in this heat? I mean the vehicles have AC, right?"

Pupil 311 is not thinking about his defiance, or even answering. No, he is thinking about how much Pupil 315 reminds him of a young Teecher. He never had such thoughts before. But, if he pictured it real hard, he could see a young Teecher sitting before him.

Pupil 315 stops waiting for a reply, turns away with a snicker.

Finally, Pupil 311 speaks. "You should be ready for anything." Then something in him, like an inspiration from the unknown passionate depths of the soul shoots out of his mouth in the form of words. "Things may change when you become Hunter. You may learn new things about White Hunters, the Empire, heck, even life when you finally make that transition."

Pupil 315 seems almost accosted. "OK," he answers.

Almost as if snapping out of it, Pupil 311 begins again, "But, after big brothering a few kids in here, I know one thing for sure, which is: you are going to be exactly what the Academy expects you to be as a White Hunter."

Pupil 315 seems shocked, is a loss for words.

Pupil 311 rises from the table. "Well, I have a lot to do getting ready and all—"

"Thank you," Pupil 315 interrupts as he jumps to his feet.

Pupil 311 doesn't expect the words.

"Thank you for saying that about me." Pupil 315 stands straight and stoic as usual. "I look forward your assent up the Temple stairs."

"Thank you," Pupil 311 replies.

The young Pupil 315 almost rushes back into the cold air of the Hunter Academy.

Pupil 311 looks up at the burning orange sky.

5

Tysheka finally reaches the top of the great Atlantic Hill. She looks out into the horizon, the Empire city below, the vast gnarled forest to the East, the great river and wasteland to the West.

She pushes the red record button on her recorder and begins to speak. "Compared to the level ground below me, I feel more like I am on top of a mountain than a hill. But, regardless of geological definitions, it was named Atlantic Hill because you could see all the way to the ocean on a clear day."

Tysheka pushes pause on her recorder. She drops her backpack to the ground, unzips it, and pulls out a book entitled, "The Meaning of Life." She looks at the crisp hardcover.

"Meaning of Empire life more like it," she says as she tosses the book down into a pit. Then she reveals a bottle of accelerant from her pack and squirts it onto the book. She lights a match and tosses it into the pit, catching the book on fire.

Empire crowds begin to roar in the distance.

Tysheka pushes pause again to begin recording. "Still on my hunt for the meaning of it all..."

11

The Temple

1

An Empire city of great buildings and structures rises from the thick green jungle wilderness of large rooted trees and vegetation. The buildings are grand, yet built in a fashion remnant of an ancient civilization.

Inside the city a roar of thousands of cheering voices rings out. Countless citizens have filled up the main walkway and courtyard in the downtown center, all here to see the new Hunter take the sacred walk to the Temple with his teacher.

"And we are here!" A female reporter corresponds from a media center table at the helm of the courtyard, her voice booming throughout the entire city. Several production staff face cameras at her. "Shevon Jones reporting for ya at the 311th White Hunter Temple Sanctification!"

The Empire roars.

"As we await the arrival of Pupil 311 and Teecher, we have a treat for the viewers. In the spirit of not only this Holy day, but with the Bicentennial Above Ground Celebration coming up, we have Empire cultural expert Peaches Washington to give us some commentary regarding the social, historical, and cultural meaning and significance of today's glorious event. Peaches?"

The camera switches to a dark middle-aged woman with extravagant braids on top of her head that rise far above her.

The woman smiles, showing large pearly white teeth. "Thank you for having me. Hello Empire!"

The masses scream hello back to her.

"It seems like forever since we have had a new White Hunter," the reporter says to Peaches.

"It's been 36 months exactly Shevon," Peaches replies. "Do you know there was a time during the Great Wars and Extermination that several Hunters a week would be anointed?"

The Empire wows.

"Yet," Peaches goes on, "We are blessed to be born during this time, where we live in a safe civilization with clear goals geared toward the people!"

The crowds roar once again.

"The lack of stress, crime, violence, and war that was present in the societies of the past will never be an issue for the Empire. Just as DeShawn teaches us, the world should not even consider these apparitions as relevant or real at all. We are very lucky to have one goal for our citizens and their lives, and that is fun, festivities, and pleasure."

The citizens around the Empire show their agreement.

The reporter asks, "Can you give us a little of the horror that societies went through in the past?"

"For instance," Peaches obliges instantly, "In the past, there was two types of war. There was the physically violent war, causing death and destruction. Yet, even within societies themselves, when there was no physical war going on at all, another type of war was always raging. It was called political war."

The reporter gasps.

"Political war referred to the system of leadership societies had before the bomb. It involved individuals with often short spans of government control, utilizing lies, theft, and other crimes against society to make personal or financial gain."

Everyone boos. The reporter looks disgusted and shakes her head.

The reporter asks her guest, "So you would say our customs are much better setup than some man or woman suddenly becoming leader?"

"Well, I would say so," Peaches agrees before elaborating. "And everyone in the Empire would agree with me. Each of our Kings are the direct descendant of DeShawn himself. Our royalty is chosen through genetic Holy Divination. The process will likely go on forever."

"Amen," the reporter states.

Peaches goes on passionately. "In the system of the Empire there is no reason anyone would yearn for such desires, as everything we could ever want is given to us from birth to death. Each of us receives 475 credits on the 1st of each month, accessible via our every so convenient barcode tattoos on our wrists, and the Bar Improvement Act of 75 gave us an additional 100 credits solely for use in bar establishments. And all of these necessities are all geared toward having fun, pleasure, all of the time."

"But what about farming? Many don't think it is fun at all," the reporter says as if she hopes she didn't just get into trouble.

"The only task citizens have had to perform is growing or raising their own food, which stems from our survival underground," Peaches pleas. "Citizens need to realize the importance that indoor lighting was for our people's survival. Now, although we walk the Earth, she still has yet to recover in a way to be able to significantly farm outdoors. Thus, indoor farming is still essential."

"Mmmmm," the reporter replies.

Peaches shakes her head and continues. "Anyways, the task of farming has now been nullified by automated hydroponic growing technology, which the government has given each Empire household a rebate for. This gives citizens even more time for fun, festivities, and pleasure."

"That is true!" The reporter chimes in happily. "I love my system! Just visit it twice a day to take a look and pick some food! Thank you Peaches for your interesting commentary."

"Thank you for having me," Peaches replies.

The reporter shifts in her seat. "Now we will make some announcements because Pupil 311 and Teecher have begun their trip down the promenade and will be here any moment!"

The crowds roar again.

"First, that agricultural genius, Hunter 281, known as Gardner, has once again brought to us new fruits and vegetables! And there will be a festival celebrating these new foods next Friday!"

The masses throughout the Empire celebrate.

"Each citizen will receive four shares of each food a week until the household has flowered each successfully for two cycles or until mass production outdoor is achieved. Next week seeds will be dispersed at 7 per household, per week, indefinitely. Now, in understanding that none of us may know what these fruits and vegetables are, and thus have no idea what they taste like, we will read what they were called in societies of the past, as well as a brief description."

Suddenly, the atmosphere of a million booming vocal sound vibrations disappear and all is quiet throughout the Empire. Everyone awaits the names of the new foods they get to try, to savor, even if each citizen will only receive a small amount of the new foods at first.

The reporter begins reading the card excitedly. "Squash, a vegetable that is much like the pumpkin!"

The Empire is roaring again.

The reporter reads the next and looks even more excited. "Carrot, a vegetable that is unlike any other. Orange, thin, and it says here indescribable in taste!"

The Empire screams with their eager palettes.

"There's one more! The fruit!" The reporter beams into the camera. "I am proud and honored to present to you a fruit we all heard about from our mommas. The fruit, with an emphasis on the we. The fruit that signified our people, our women, we have perfected–"

A drum roll sounds,

"The legend, no, the real thing, the real deal," the reporter shouts, "the peach!"

The crowds go crazy! Mass hysteria hits everyone. People jump up and down, pull their hair out, and drop to the ground in convulsions.

The reporter dances on top of her media table.

Suddenly, a parade of hip-hop musicians enters the courtyard.

The reporter jumps down from the table and gets back into her chair. "The ceremony has begun!"

Pupil 311 and Teecher follow the parade. They slowly walk down the courtyard and stop before the grand stairs to the Temple of Sanctification.

"Pupil 311 and his famous trainer Teecher are about to begin that Holy climb to the Temple of Sanctification!" the reporter announces.

The crowds scream in approval again.

Cameras posted in all crannies of the courtyard broadcast throughout the Empire. All Empire screens show Pupil 311 and Teecher, standing at the bottom of the high Temple staircase.

Every dark face is watching the two figures at the Temple stairs.

Pupil 311 stares in awe at the stairs before him, then up to the doors of the Romanesque building sitting atop. He has always hoped this day would come, but the mystery of not knowing was the worst for him. Other recruits and even the boys in the old neighborhood he lived in would always create stories of what lay beyond those Temple doors.

"Relax" Teecher tells him.

Pupil 311 sees that his teacher is watching him. "I will, yes sir."

Teecher snickers at him. "This is merely ceremonial. A formality."

Pupil 311 nods, but doesn't understand.

"Are you ready?" Teecher asks.

"Yes, my Teecher," the pupil responds.

Pupil 311 and Teecher begin to ascend the steps.

The citizens roar even louder. A huge circle of royal workers lining the giant downtown courtyard throw flower petals and let doves fly into the air.

Teecher and Pupil 311 climb the charred black steps toward the temple. The sky above them seems to be an even more scorching orange as an intense heat beats down from a glowing sun.

As the two ascend Teecher looks over at Pupil 311. "You are a very lucky person Pupil, I want to know that you truly understand that. Most citizens of the Colored Empire never get to do anything at all with their lives. You may not understand it as you have lived in the training center most your entire life, but society truly doesn't need anything except us. There are no jobs, no roles, no purposes, only existence."

Pupil 311 keeps his gaze forward. "I know these things my Teecher."

"But I don't know if you really understand," Teecher responds. "Not yet. Not truly yet."

From their height, Pupil 311 notices the toddler training courtyard where small troupes of 5 and 6-year old Hunters are trained with the old toy spear. Again thoughts of his youth at the Academy, and the fact he was at the end of all of it. Now a Hunter, something altogether different.

Teecher becomes angry suddenly. "Well, I tell you son, of the many Hunters I have trained you are not the most enthused. We are walking the grand staircase to your ceremonial Sanctification and you seem off somewhere else."

Pupil 311 snaps out of his youth memories, finally turning his gaze toward Teecher. "I am sorry my Teecher. I am just, um, a little anxious about it all."

Teecher still is openly displeased.

Pupil 311 sees this and goes on, "I mean, like you said, it is my Sanctification, and I am beginning a new life."

"That you are." Teecher grins at his student, then a light comes to his old hawk-like eyes.

The young pupil now stares ahead as expected.

"Yes, I remember being young, imagining what it would be like." Teecher looks ahead now. "Perhaps, I was a little out of it myself." Teecher begins to reminisce. "I was such a young scrapper. The kingdom was brand new then! The Great Wars were over and the Extermination had begun."

"We are here my Teecher," Pupil 311 announces.

Teecher realizes they have reached the top of the steps, grabs his student's arm firmly, pulling him in close. "This is nothing my Pupil," he hisses with excitement. "Tonight your first kill is your true sanctification."

Pupil 311's face is filled with fear now. He begins to ask, "Do you think we will ever see another-?"

"Let us finish your climb, Pupil 311," Teecher interrupts and waves him up.

The young Hunter nods in obedience.

The two climb the last step together and face the two giant wooden doors. The words "The Temple of Sanctification" are engraved over the entrance.

Pupil 311 immediately analyzes the door's countless intricately carved images of their people's culture and beliefs. He notices depictions of tales he learned as a child. His eyes freeze on a detailed engraving of the Bacalou, the boogie beast that scared the children growing up more than the nightmarish idea of hordes of bloodthirsty whites. The monster's eyes seem all too real, staring at him, the mouth open to show the beast's countless razor sharp teeth.

Teecher pulls the giant doors open and Pupil 311 sighs in relief as the Bacalou's piercing eyes cannot stare at him any longer. The doors both make a loud hoarse creek as they slowly move to reveal a dark dank stairway.

The crowd cheers in unison once again.

Pupil 311 is frozen in fear and wonderment as Teecher motions for him to enter the ancient Temple.

"Do not fear my pupil. No living thing exists within this Temple cave." He motions for him once again.

The pupil finally obeys, joining Teecher in the Temple entrance.

Inside the dark and narrow stairway the two descend toward a dim light below.

Teecher puts his arm around his student. "Most citizens of the City of Colored never get to see what you are about to. The Bible is conveyed through tongue by our people. But as a White Hunter you have access to the real thing."

Pupil 311 walks with Teecher to an iron door of an age-old bunker. Teecher approaches the door and bends close to the wall. There a dim light shows the numbers of a keypad. A few taps from Teecher's fingertips on the numbers make the bunker door open partially, releasing a gush of old air.

"Here we are," Teecher declares as he pries the door open the rest of the way and ushers his student in. Once in, Teecher marches past his pupil to a set of switches, hits several, the entire area becomes lit up by multiple 20th century HID lights that line the cave walls. Teecher points up toward the wall. "Any questions you have can be answered by the Bible." The lights now illuminate the cave wall. On it is a giant intricate hand drawn mural. Its colors are dulled from being in the dank darkness of the cave, but the images are as real as the two standing before them. A semi-English text is engraved below the beautiful scenes.

"The Bible Wall!" Pupil 311 exclaims. He stares at the wall in astonishment.

Teecher points at the first mural. It depicts the first man and woman as dark brown skinned. "From the beginning, when Godallah created the first man, and later woman, to live in paradise."

Below the first people are two brown skinned brothers in paradise with their parents and many different types of animals.

Teecher goes on. "Godallah bestowed two sons upon them. Yet, one of their sons became jealous of his brother and struck him down."

Teecher points to the next mural. One brother stands over the other, wild-eyed, stone in hand, with blood everywhere. "Godallah was angered by his sin, cast him from his people, and marked his face forever."

The following mural shows the brother, now white, being cast from his parents by a great light.

Teecher stands up rather straight as if about to salute, then belts out, "His offspring would forever be marked so that Godallah's people would merely need to look upon their face to know the innate instinct of sadism that lies within each of them."

Pupil 311 knew the verses. But he still could not get it out of his head that they aren't fairy tales. After seeing his first white last night, and then his death, Pupil 311 was still in some sort of shock, feeling numb about his life at this point. Furthermore, at around two AM the previous night he had woken up in a cold sweat with the painful and lasting feeling of guilt, perhaps had a bad dream about it. And he was thankful that he remembered nothing about his dreams that night.

When 311 first pondered the fact that whites existed, he thought of the childhood fears he had about whites, how adults would use them to scare the kids, and the verses they all had to learn. But in the morning these fears, despite the helpless state of the old white man he encountered, had blossomed into a sense of terror regarding life in general.

Pupil 311 thinks about of all this as he stares through the mural, knowing nothing would be the same in this world.

Teecher is still caught up with his sanctification speech. "Though we all know man failed to stop the cursed race from their ultimate cause in conquering the world." Pupil 311's attention is drawn to the next mural, which is much bigger than the others. In it, a giant mushroom cloud explodes into fiery orange, pushing the blue sky back and away into black.

Teecher saunters to the mural to continue the Bible story. "And ultimately the whites almost destroyed Earth."

At the bottom of the mushroom cloud skyscrapers shrivel and water boils. "Their attempts to reach Godallah in their buildings to the Heavens were destroyed by their own evil wars," Teecher exclaims. "And if not for our prophet Deshawn, who took us into the ground for enough generations, we would have surely perished!"

The next mural shows a black man leading a huge group of other dark skinned people into some sort of cave. He is wearing a long purple robe and has dreadlocks and sunglasses on.

Teecher points to the next depiction. "Our scientists waited for the radiation levels to lower, and by the will of Godallah, our people rose from the ground to dwell upon the Earth once again. After our return above ground whites were encountered rather quickly and conflicts began." The mural shows a battle, large units of blacks attacking nearby villages of whites. "This began the Great Wars which resulted in the eradication of the white settlements."

In the corners of the picture several whites flee into hiding, some toward the forest, some to the wasteland, but all are tracked by White Hunters. "Once the groups were destroyed the need for the Order of White Hunters was apparent. The Great Extermination then began."

Teecher glances back at his student proudly. "And that is how we were born."

Pupil 311 nods and proceeds to the final mural. It is different as it has no figures, just two stone tablets containing a multitude of writing. Pupil 311's eyes widen. "The law!"

Teecher stands proud. "Yes. Some passages of importance here: 1. There is only the progression of the black race and the destruction of the white race. 11. Godallah cursed the whites, for it is them that destroyed the Earth twice before, and it is the duty of the enlightened black man to do all to prevent the white's control of the world again. 25. The white race will conquer, it is in their nature."

The two study the words.

Pupil 311 gets closer to the wall, inspecting the texture carefully.

"So," Teecher concludes, "Now you have seen the Bible Wall and read the law in person."

Pupil 311 backs away from the wall into attention stance. "So what now?"

Teecher smiles. "Well, now, I, and everyone else, begin to call you by a different name. Though you will always better your skills and retain knowledge, you are no longer a Pupil. You are now Hunter 311."

The new Hunter is speechless. Hunter 311 takes a breath and shows a small smile. "I've been training, waiting, dreaming about this my entire life."

Teecher nods, still smiling. "As the law states you have become a Hunter because I have trained you as much as I can and because you have passed all the skill tests required by a Hunter."

Hunter 311 thinks for a moment before looking to Teecher. "But what now Teecher?"

Teecher's smile grows even bigger. "You will see young Hunter 311."

2

The thousands roar again as the temple doors slowly swing back open. Teecher and Hunter 311 emerge from the sacred darkness.

The old Hunter raises his hand to quiet the masses. After a moment the cheers die down and Teecher begins to speak. "The transformation has occurred! Pupil 311 is now Hunter 311!"

The crowd roars once again.

Teecher and Hunter 311 descend back down the many steps, waving to the crowd.

The old man studies his transformed student. "What will you do until tomorrow?"

Hunter 311 only thinks for a moment. "Visit my niece."

Teecher nods, still waving.

Hunter 311 realizes he stopped waving, jolts his hand up to wave again. "Perhaps visit with Hunter 281."

Teecher almost stops, displeased. "Most call him Gardener."

Hunter 311 tries to respectfully defend him. "Yet, is it not true this is not his given title, like Teecher has been in your case?"

Teecher seems to ignore the comment about his name. "What reason are you to meet with him?"

Hunter 311 suddenly feels the urge, the courage, to talk speak openly. "We have been friends for years, don't you know?"

Teecher grunts. "No, I didn't."

Silence for a few moments as the two make their way to the last set of steps.

"Showing you good tips on gardening is he?"

"Actually, yes he does," Hunter 311 smiles.

"Speak of the Gardener," Teecher eyes Gardner in the front row of the crowd.

Hunter 311 sees him as well. "Everyone is here." He sees the entire Hunter fleet, the elders, as well as the Pupils. He spots Pupil 315, the young brother giving him an affirmative nod.

Banners unfold all over the courtyard with huge pictures of Hunter 311 and his name in bold.

Teecher is still locked onto Gardner with his piercing stare. "Are you to go with him now?" he asks.

Hunter 311 remembers what he got himself into and begins to regret venturing to speak so openly suddenly. "We have plans to conversate. He is a very smart man and is willing to teach rare knowledge. You always taught me to take on any knowledge you can, to become a well-rounded Hunter."

Teecher scowls. "Useful knowledge." He studies his new found Hunter seriously before lighting up. "Well, it isn't knowledge you would get from me!" He smacks Hunter 311 on the back and laughs.

Hunter 311 looks at Teecher, seeing the same presentation he saw every day of his training life, not a caring teacher willing to respect and care for his student, but instead an image of ignorant power, nothing but an old oversized bully. But the new Hunter would never be that bold to venture saying such thoughts, especially after the awkwardness Gardner just created.

When the two finally reach the ground, the crowd roars even louder.

"Just wave," Teecher orders.

3

"I've never really noticed, but your brother is hot," Monique tells Cicily.

Crystal shakes her head.

"I know," Cicily replies, "He would have been some ladies' man if he didn't have the life of a Hunter."

Hunter 311 and Teecher stand before the Empire, broadcasted to every screen in the land, waving to all.

"He finally made it," Cicily gazes at her brother. Images of childhood memories flood her mind, at first normal happy times of play and adventure, then the spoiled pictures always come, of the government arriving at her house, talking to her parents, and taking away her little brother.

Cicily remembers her father saying, "Be proud my love, only a fraction of citizens of the Empire ever get to know such a life, such an exciting life full of purpose!" Then he would go into stories of how he imagined being a Hunter as a child, playing whites and hunters with his neighborhood friends.

But, for whatever reason, due to her feminine natural inclinations which often were quick to disregard masculine wiles such as Hunting, or because the innate existence of love for a sibling, it was the one trauma of her childhood that she would always hold with her.

Hunter 311 and Teecher shake hands on screen. The Empire city trolley pulls up and the two climb inside.

"I am very proud of him," Cicily declares to her two best friends.

"I am too," Crystal says.

"Of course," Monique acknowledges. "Beats my brother, the wanna-be pimp living with his mother still," she smirks.

"The Empires is full of wanna-be pimps," Crystal laughs.

"That's my point," Monique replies, "Only good for one thing." She pokes a hole in her cheek a couple of times.

"You're sick!" Crystal tells her.

Monique puts her hand on her head. "I don't feel warm." She laughs.

"It's party time!" a man's voice booms. A light skinned man's face fills all the screens in the place. He flashes his array of gold teeth before introducing himself. "I am Don Ghostliani! And it is time!" The camera pulls back as he dances, his red silk outfit shines as he spins.

The theater roars in approval.

"I love this song!" Monique cheers.

"Party time is now," Don Ghostliani begins to rap.

Cicily motions for an aisle waiter. A short dark waiter sees her but stays still. "Could we get another round of drinks?" Cicily calls out to him, "Two gin and juices, a Hennessey, and NizzeCola chasers?"

Several people sitting in nearby rows are now watching and listening.

"Why don't you calm down?" Crystal touches Cicily's arm.

Cicily pulls away. "I know the consequences, I don't care! They never took his name away in my eyes."

Monique and Crystal look around.

"Never had a childhood," Crystal mutters before taking a huge swallow of her drink.

"Everything is OK here," Crystal informs the patrons staring, "Just a little too much to drink." She smiles before putting her attention back to Cicily. "You gonna be OK Cil?"

Cicily stares down at the table for a few seconds before looking at Crystal and telling her, "I don't think anything will ever be fine again."

4

Gardner lets out a laugh as he scans his palm to open the Hunter Agriculture security doors.

"Ya, he never did like me," Gardner opens the door and ushers Hunter 311 in. "Your Teecher, along with all the other young Hunters, liked to put me in the trash can for fun."

"What?" Hunter 311 shakes his head. "You know that sounds so believable."

Gardner leads Hunter 311 into the warehouses. "I saw him looking at me as you two were coming down the last steps."

"I decided to mention our friendship," Hunter 311 says.

Gardner is intrigued. "And it's length?"

Hunter 311 nods.

Gardner laughs again. "Boy, I bet he was so pissed that he never found out through his highly impeccable detective skill set or his machoistic associates he calls friends."

Hunter 311 laughs now as well. "I think you could say that. He showed a different side to his usual disgust."

"He believes I serve no real purpose." Gardner approaches the Greenhouse doors, they slide open automatically. "Or that if I do serve a purpose, it is one for a citizen, not a Hunter."

Gardner enters the Greenhouse and Hunter 311 follows. The Hunter Greenhouse is a gigantic dome warehouse housing an array of the vegetables, fruits, and herbs consumed by the Hunters and Pupils at the academy.

The enormous space is packed full of rows of hydroponics, each on a continuously fed line of nutrients. Each section consists of a multitude of flourishing above ground plants. An enormous track of LED lights constantly roam the ceiling in order to soak all possible spaces with nutritious light.

"You know the two main warehouses very well, given that you have been coming here since you were a child." Gardner passes the strawberries, blackberries, and peppers.

"Some of the best times of my childhood," Hunter 311 says below his breath.

Gardner seems to almost hear it. "And the fact that I have had to keep it to myself that you were at the heart of many of the agricultural unit's triumphs over the years has been too much."

Hunter 311 tries to ignore him as the two enter a second warehouse.

"This entire unit is because of you," Gardner says. "Without all your work, your hypothesis regarding indoor soil grows and environmental controls, and all your wild ideas, we would never have grown fruit such as oranges and bananas. If it wasn't for you this agricultural unit itself would not be the place where the Empire has been trying re-jumpstart different kinds of fruit and vegetables that were either not taken below by their ancestors, or did not survive somehow. It couldn't be where Empire scientists are working on solving the fertility of the soil and growth issues with plants and trees due to the effects of radiation."

Hunter 311 peers out into the multitude of lines of vegetable and fruit trees filling the second warehouse as if not even listening to Gardner's ramble. He follows the LED lights rotate around the room.

"I would prefer we still keep all that between us," Hunter 311 states. "No one passing around awards or merits to a Hunter for such activities."

Gardner smirks.

Hunter 311 realizes he may have disrespected the old farming Hunter. "I didn't mean-"

Gardner raises his head for silence. "No need to, I understand what you are saying."

Gardner leads Hunter 311 to another set of larger security doors in the back of the warehouse. He raises his hand toward the scanner, but stops and turns to Hunter 311. "So Teecher must of realized why you'd be so eager to meet with me right after your graduation to Hunter."

"I think he did," Hunter 311 replies.

Gardner stares at him, smiling.

"Come on!" Hunter 311 blurts.

Gardner snaps out of it, "Oh ya."

"I have been waiting for this since I was 13!" Hunter 311 steps toward the doors.

Gardner scans his hand, the doors whishes open, and the pungent smell hits both men in the face.

Inside is a vast sea of green, sparkling, sticky buds.

"Halleluiah!" Hunter 311 exclaims. He rushes in and drops to his knees. "Sweet Lord in Heaven!"

"Now calm down!" Gardner yells, running in after him.

5

"And that concludes our coverage of the graduation of our Empire's 311th White Hunter!" a mechanical voice booms. "May Godallah be with him and the Empire!"

The Public Theater screens switch to a soap opera.

"That's why we came home two days early for Norlins?" Monique asks as she adjusts her bra to show off her breasts as much as possible.

"How on Earth have we stayed friends with you all these years?" Crystal asks. "You know Cicily needed to see her brother's graduation."

"On screens? We could have done that from some bar on Bourbon Street!"

"Just shut up Monique," Crystal snaps.

"She has a point," Cicily states dryly. "There wasn't much to watching that."

"Let's go to the game," suddenly Monique says excitedly.

Crystal seems unsure, looks at Cicily.

Cicily finishes her drink. "Why not?" She concludes.

The three get up from their table and leave the Public Theater.

6

Pupil 315 enters the Pupil dormitory, the metal doors slide closed behind him.

"How was your one on one?" Pupil 316 asks him. He sits with his brother at one of the community tables.

"Nothing special," he answers insipidly.

"You seemed to be in a good mood at the Temple ceremony," Pupil 317 adds.

"Don't watch me," Pupil 315 snarls.

"Boy, I can't wait to walk the steps like 311 just did!" Hunter 318 exclaims.

"That's if you make it," Pupil 315 jeers. "And as of right now, I am not too sure."

The 5-year old is hurt, he begins to sniffle.

"Leave him alone," Pupil 316 demands.

"Leave him alone!" Pupil 315 mocks his voice. "Look, I am not sure about you two either, and you've been here for years!"

They all are hurt now.

Pupil 315 wags his finger at them. "I am going to get some dinner and go to bed. I don't want to hear anything from you little punks the rest of the night. Got it?"

They all answer with their silence.

7

"I hope you realize the importance of this plant," Gardner says.

Hunter 311 is dumbfounded. "Of course I do!" He looks at the sea of buds as if in love with each plant.

"And its variety of uses!" Gardner snaps Hunter 311 out of his love locked daydream. "Even after harvesting the buds and crystal extraction, the plant has vital uses in paper, textile, and fuel industries. I mean we have harnessed so much from them. And so much because of you and your experiments!"

Hunter 311 stares out into space. "You know it all started when I got two different batches."

"Yes, I know the story—"

Hunter 311 goes on as Gardner is not even there. "You gave me Afghani and Haze. And I could tell the Afghani was much more of a low feeling, like alcohol almost, while the Haze was more of an uplifting, almost transparent high."

Gardner begins to speak again, but waves off the idea.

"So I knew that there was some natural inclination to bring about these effects, and I knew it was because variation in the properties of potency in the plant. So I came back here and altered my grow." Hunter 311 stands and grabs a bud from a tall plant.

"Be careful!" Gardner pleas.

Hunter 311 lets the bud spring free and goes on. "Since I had just finished my experiments on trichomes, I already knew that these strands reached maximum THC potency at different times. The Afghani, from the Indica part of the world, tended to show trichome degeneration and THC potency earlier than the Sativa plants did."

"So if a grower created a standard grow time of 9 weeks, then Sativa trichomes would degenerate, turning from white to brownish gold, into another newly found psychoreactive chemical called CBD," Gardner finished for him.

Hunter 311 smiles proudly. "That's right."

"And so you realized you could make stony Sativa and super-stony Indica simply by letting the trichomes degenerate," Gardner pats Hunter 311 on the back.

"Simply, another level of control," Hunter 311 says.

8

Cicily, Crystal, and Monique approach the B-Ball arena.

"I've been waiting for these two teams to play each other!" Monique exclaims. "I have to put on my fan gear!" She reaches inside her purse and reveals her makeup coordinator. She punches something into the handheld computer and instantly green face paint appears all over her face, the word "PLAYERS" in bold on her forehead.

"You are too much," Crystal tells her.

"Come on!" Monique races to the entrance.

Cicily shakes her head. "I don't know what she loves more: sex or the Players B-Ball team!"

"Let's not lose her," Crystal urges.

"Yes, I don't want to spend the entire time looking for her," Cicily answers as the two enter the payment turnstile.

Cicily slides her barcode tattoo over the payment reader. The light on the reader goes red.

"Insufficient funds!" the mechanical voice of the payment reader blurts out.

Cicily cannot believe it. She slides her hand again, same red light and message.

"He must have put everything on my bill!" Crystal begins to cry.

"It's OK," Crystal swoops in and scans her hand twice, then ushers her into the stadium. "He's gone, let's go have some fun."

Cicily shakes her head, but actually takes her friend's advice, smiles, and says, "Where is Monique? You know we can't have fun without being able to make fun of her."

Crystal laughs, happy to see Cicily try to feel better. "I bet she is at the bar."

"To the bar we go," Cicily declares.

The mechanical B-Ball announcement voice booms over the countless stadium speakers. "And we are gathered here for a match-up with the intense Buckhead Big Bucks versus the Midtown Players!"

"Hey girls!" Monique calls out from a row of seats.

"She's not at the bar," Cicily points out. "It's a miracle."

"And no men either," Crystal adds.

"Shut up!" Monique already sits under the hair permer in her spectator seat. "I've been dying to change my look this week." She punches a few digits into her seat's number pad and a NizzeCola and hotdog shoot from the back of the seat in front of her.

The two other women sit in their seats.

"You gonna do anything drastic?" Crystal asks Cicily.

Cicily pushes the button for the hair dome to come down. "I am really thinking about it." She logs into her seat's screen and begins looking at different hairstyles on her on an image of her face and head. She stops at a wild old-school African haircut, sees the 50 credit price tag and remembers the red light and annoying voice at the entrance.

"It's OK," Crystal scans her hand on Cicily's seat scanner, 50 credits show up on her screen.

"You didn't have to do that," Cicily protests.

"You don't have to do much in the Empire. Grow your own maybe." Crystal smiles. "I wanted to."

"Thank you. I love you girl." Cicily smiles at Crystal before skipping another few hairstyles and choosing the classic T-Boz cut and coloring for only 30 credits. "Look, I can give you change."

"And it looks so good on you," Crystal comments on Cicily's image on screen.

"We will see the result soon!" Cicily calls out as the dome begins to hum and vibrate. In a second it rises, revealing the entirely new haircut, produced in only moments.

"Looks good," Crystal says.

Monique nods as she takes a bite of her dog. Her dome suddenly stops humming and rises as well.

"Whoa girl!" Crystal blurts out.

Monique's short hair has turned to very long, frizzy locks, ever so light and wavy in the air. "How do you like it?"

Cicily and Crystal study her for a few moments, both end up speechless.

"I know it looks good," Monique puts her hand out at them. "Anyway, I am going to test this at the bar right now." Monique quickly gets up and rushes to the bar entrance.

Cicily looks at Crystal. "Are you going to do something to your hair?"

"Maybe my nails," Crystal says inspecting them. They are long and lavishly painted red.

"Tip off in 2 minutes!" the B-Ball mechanical announcer booms through the stadium.

9

Hunter 311 and Gardner stand on the Hunter Academy steps.

Gardner stares at Hunter 311. "I hope you are ready for this new life."

Hunter 311 looks out onto the city. "I hope so as well." He realizes Gardner is staring at him, and with their distance being so close, he steps away. "I mean, nothing goes on anymore for us Hunters. You know that."

Images flood his mind. Of the white man, the chase, the weapons, the fear, the blood, and Teecher's menacing stare, cold eyes, like a robot.

"They don't show up anymore, do they?" Gardner says with a strange look on his face.

Hunter 311 avoids looking at Gardner, he begins to speak Hunter motto. "That is proof in the power and purpose of the White Hunters."

Gardner slaps Hunter 311 on the back. "Ya, sure it is."

Hunter 311 is unsure what to think or do except depart. "OK. See you soon my friend." He walks away, Gardner staring at him until he disappears.

10

"Go Playas!" Monique screams as she waves her Playas banner all around. Her new kinky haircut bounces around with her.

"Is she for real?" a woman nearby asks aloud.

"Watch it bitch," Cicily tells her seriously.

The woman turns back to the game without a word.

"Stupid hoes," Crystal comments. She punches in for two NizzeColas, the door on the back of the chair in front of her slides up and the mechanical tray juts out with the two beverages. She hands one to Cicily.

"Thank you," Cicily says.

"Foul on Playas!" the B-Ball mechanical announcer declares.

More than half the crowd screams in protest.

"Bad call! Bad Call!" Monique screams at the top of her lungs.

The giant scoreboard shows 976 - 976.

On the court the referee hands the B-Ball to number 45 of Cash Bucks. He is beaten and bloody. He approaches the free throw line, bounces the ball twice, and shoots it through the hoop.

The crowd roars again. The scoreboard changes to 976 - 980.

"No! No!" Monique shouts as she stomps her feet on the ground.

Number 45 falls back to the opposite side of the court to defend, while number 89 of the Playas grabs the B-Ball. He too is bloodied, nose crooked, busted lip. He passes to number 101 who dribbles twice while limping on his left leg, both eyes blackened, but quickly passes back to number 89.

But, number 45 comes from behind to try and pick the ball from player 89. Just as number 45 gets within guarding distance of him, player 89 begins to throw punches and elbows. Two strike number 45 in the face, one right in the chin. He goes down hard, hitting the court with a thud.

"Knockout! Knockout!" the mechanical B-Ball announcer calls out.

The crowd roars.

"Shit no!" Monique curses. "No, no!"

The giant scoreboard lights up: Final Score! 976-990!

"The Midtown Playas have lost their last teammate in Darius Johnson, number 45, taken out with a violent series of punches and elbows when trying to guard Tyrone Black, number 89 of the Cash Bucks!"

Tyrone Black stands in the middle of the court with his hands raised. His teammates celebrate around him.

"That is Black's 47th knockout in professional B-Ball!" The B-Ball announcer declares. "Two more and he will tie the world record, currently held by Andre Williams, who retired nearly five years ago!"

People begin to pour out of the stadium at an alarming rate.

Cicily and Crystal do not seem to care as much as many others.

"Let me see your nails girl," Cicily says.

Crystal shows her new purple nails with stone trim.

Cicily looks at them closely. "Beautiful girl, beautiful."

"Let's get out of here," Monique snaps, her face paint already gone. "Shitty day."

"Don't be a sore loser," Crystal pokes Monique.

"Stop," Monique orders her away. "I need a drink." She storms away.

Cicily and Crystal smile at each before following her.

11

Hunter 311, on Cloud 9, struts proudly down a city street.

An automated advertisement beams up a building wall. "Give Norlins a try! What happens in Norlins stays in Norlins!" The commercial shows a man dressed lavishly in front of a Norlins hotspot. "It's the empire outside the Empire! Trip bundles starting at 150 credits!"

Hunter 311 passes the advertisement and turns on a side street. He walks only a few feet before stopping at address 747007987. He enters the large unlocked oak door. Once inside, he calls out, "Cicily? Tysheka? You guys around?"

"Uncle!" a little girl's voice emanates from the single bedroom in the back of the tiny apartment. Tysheka emerges in mid run, jumping into her uncle's arms. The two hug, but Tysheka breaks free slightly. "I cannot believe you got to go to the Temple finally!"

Hunter 311 smiles, trying to keep his pride hidden from his young niece. "Yes, I did."

"So," Tysheka speaks to her uncle almost as he were a child. "You are not a Pupil anymore!"

Hunter 311 takes a step back, salutes. "I am now called Hunter 311."

"Ya," Tysheka replies, "I saw your graduation from the best seat in the Empire."

"From where?" Hunter 311 asks with a smile.

"On Atlantic Hill."

"Way up there?" Hunter 311 is astonished she would venture that far from the city. "When did you start going out there?"

"I have been for years now." Tysheka opens the digital phone screen and checks her messages.

"You have no new messages," the phone tells her.

Tysheka turns back to her uncle. "So Hunter 311?" Tysheka thinks about the name, studies her uncle. "I am going to call you just 311."

"Whatever you want sweetie," Hunter 311 replies with a smile. "Where's your mother?"

Tysheka looks down, sullen. "At least she's not at the club again," she answers her uncle finally. "She is somewhere with her friends. They just came back from Norlins."

Hunter 311 is angry. It's just like his sister. He shakes his head thinking about the problem he has been dealing with since his niece was born.

"I just saw one of those bloodsucking advertisements for trips there," he says as he enters the kitchen nook. "Let's have some dinner, maybe she will show up while we eat."

Tysheka skips to the fridge, opens it and looks inside. The small unit is empty.

Hunter 311 frowns. "The cabinet look like this too?"

Tysheka shakes her head "yes."

"My sister!" Hunter 311 walks to a door in the kitchen space and swings it open. Inside is a large room with rows of rain gutters lining the floor, high pressure sodium bulbs hovering over. He takes a look around saying, "You guys don't even have any rockwool!"

Tysheka joins her uncle. "She has not grown anything for months uncle."

Hunter 311 is furious. "And what happened to the automatic systems and LEDs I installed in here for you last year?"

His niece shrugs. "They disappeared shortly before she left for Norlins. I am pretty sure she sold them for spending money to use on her trip."

He looks into the derelict grow room. "The empire outside the Empire, they are calling it."

"I remember when Norlins was a shanty town when I was growing up," Tysheka reminisces. "They have done so much building there."

Hunter 311 grunts and shuts the grow room door. "More than here it seems. And the whole idea of making a vacation destination for the Empire is more than odd given the geological circumstances of our present time. Really, it is no more than an excuse for citizens to act without even less morals and gamble away your monthly credits if you ask me."

"Perfect place for mother then," Tysheka retorts. She thinks about what she said, feels awkward and goes on. "Anyways, I told her how valuable the automatic hydroponic systems were, how much you paid for them, I mean my friend Barbara's dad just put the same system in and it cost him over 1,000 credits. Anyways, she only used two rows and I told her if she just bought some cubes and seeds she would have extra food every week and could barter the extra with Janice at the Hairdresser. She could of got her hair and nails done every week for free!"

"I agree totally." Hunter 311 looks back at the fridge. "How have you guys been eating?"

"Momma has been getting food on loan from others. The Williams have a huge garden next door." Tysheka is uncomfortable now, her uncle notices.

"OK, honey, let's go out to eat," Hunter 311 offers.

Tysheka is overjoyed. "Yes! I love going to the Academy cafe!"

"Oh no," Hunter 311 shakes his head. "We are going to a better cafe."

Tysheka's eyes widen in realization. "You're a Hunter now! We get to go to the Hunter restaurant!"

Hunter 311 nods. "I was hoping you would guess," he laughs. "Seeing how only two places exist in the entire Empire that serve food."

Tysheka is not listening. She puts on her coat and quickly spins back around to face him. "I'm ready," she informs her uncle.

"Well, then we are off," Hunter 311 says, turning toward the door.

"Wait," Tysheka pleas. "I must leave a note for momma."

Hunter 311 smiles. "You do that sweetie, I'll pull the car around." He exits the front door of the apartment.

Tysheka approaches the tiny refrigerator, simply touches it to make a screen appear. With her finger she writes, "Dear momma, went with uncle to celebrate his becoming a Hunter, Tysheka" and touches the send button.

She thinks for a second, sullen again, where her mother is and what she is doing. But, the sound of many voices outside her apartment snaps her out of it.

Tysheka rushes out of her apartment to find her uncle bombarded by reporters and Hunter fans.

"Yes, I am very proud," Hunter is saying to the many cameras, microphones, eyes, and ears pointed at him. "But, as you know already I cannot say much more than that. Besides, I am taking my niece out to eat right now." Hunter 311 introduces Tysheka as she steps outside her front door.

For a few moments all cameras and eyes are on young Tysheka.

"So it is not a good time," Hunter 311 continues.

Tysheka is frozen by the reporter's lights and all the attention. Hunter 311 motions for her to come out.

"Taking your niece to the famed Hunter Restaurant!" a reporter yells. "Tell us what you expect young Tysheka!"

"What will you order?" another reporter calls out.

Tysheka is silent and still frozen. Finally, she seems to regain her composure and answers beautifully. "I really don't know what to expect. And I haven't seen their menu yet."

The reporters and fans laugh joyfully to her comment.

She steps down her front steps and joins her uncle at last.

"We hope," Hunter 311 looks directly into a camera in his face, "everyone at home has a good night. Godallah Bless the Empire."

Hunter 311 leads his niece away from the crowd to his Hunter vehicle. Cameras roll and eyes watch Hunter 311 open the passenger door to let Tysheka in, close it, and get in the driver's seat.

The crowd cheers and reporters begin their commentaries regarding the new White Hunter.

"I didn't realize it would be this serious," Tysheka tells her uncle.

"There has not been a new Hunter for 12-years," Hunter 311 replies as he drives toward Malcolm X Boulevard. "So you don't remember all the media coverage surrounding Hunter 310."

"No," she shakes her head.

Hunter 311 turns a corner. "I know my story can't be as media-worthy as Hunter 310's."

"Why?" Tysheka asks.

Hunter smiles naughtily. "Let's just say Pupil 310 liked the ladies too much."

Tysheka giggles. "Uncle!"

"What?" he asks in contention. "He did. I'm not making it up."

Tysheka laughs some more. "And what about you, Mr. Hunter 311?"

Hunter 311 looks as if he's been accused. "Me? What?"

Tysheka gives him the "you know" look. "When are you going to get married? Or even date?"

Hunter 311 looks away, tries to laugh it off.

"You're probably the Empire's number one catch, uncle," Tysheka tells him. "I watched Ebony last night and they named you the number one bachelor in the entire Empire."

Hunter 311 cannot believe it. He smiles for a second thinking about it, the possibilities, but then each scenario becomes not possible. "How can I be the number one bachelor if I don't know anyone but Hunters?"

Tysheka shrugs. "You know me and momma. Maybe we can introduce you to a girl."

"In your neighborhood?" Hunter 311 eyes his niece. "No thanks. Too much festival, not enough brains."

Tysheka laughs. "I know it's not the best place to live."

Hunter 311 looks forward, puts a serious look on his face. "And now that I am Hunter I plan on changing that."

Tysheka is confused. "What do you mean?"

Hunter 311 bites his lip before speaking. "I plan on finding you guys a new place." He looks at his niece. "In another part of the Empire."

Tysheka doesn't know what to say at first.

Hunter 311 makes a turn.

After a minute Tysheka finally speaks. "Look uncle, I love you so much, you know that. But you don't have to look out for us. I mean at least in the way you are talking about."

"You are my only family," he states. "Of course I have to. And I want to."

"But uncle–" Tysheka begins to protest.

"But nothing," Hunter 311 interrupts with a huge smile. "I love you. And we will talk about this later."

Tysheka shakes her head. She is about to make another point in protest when her uncle suddenly pulls the Hunter vehicle over.

"We're here!" Hunter 311 exclaims, making his niece giggle as he can so well.

Tysheka sees the crowd now; the same reporters and fans await their arrival. "They beat us here?"

Hunter 311 nods dismally. "Don't ask." He exits the vehicle, going to her side to let her out.

Cameras flash and fans cheer.

Tysheka sees the Hunter Restaurant entrance and sign, a large array of lights and robotics. "So bright," Tysheka says to her uncle.

"The food is even better I hear," he says leading her to the giant metal doors. "And after tonight, you will definitely know the menu."

12

Teecher pulls into an alley parking spot and checks the mirrors before exiting the Hunter vehicle.

"Not chasing them in this far are you?" a voice calls out.

Teecher turns to see an old man, dressed in typical senior khakis and sweater. "Hello, Mr. Turner. No, we've never had to chase any white into the city, you know that."

Teecher approaches Mr. Turner to shake his hand, but in a flash the old man grabs his forearm and holds him tight. "They will," the old man attempts to spit out his words, eyes wild. "The whites will come."

"Calm down, Mr. Turner." Teecher holds him tighter and pulls a needle from his hip satchel.

"But you don't know like my generation!" Mr. Turner begins to scream. "You hunters need to know—"

Teecher injects the old man, stopping him in mid-sentence, and lets his sleeping body down slowly before radioing in. "I have a 1-51. Need a pick up. My coordinates are confirmed. Out."

Teecher kneels down to the old man. "I am very sorry Mr. Turner."

Suddenly, a vehicle arrives, two very short men dressed in rubber white suits get out and salute Teecher.

"Do your duty," is all Teecher says.

The two men immediately reveal an old fashioned hospital bed from their vehicle, then together they hoist Mr. Turner into the bed and shove him into their vehicle. The men get back into the vehicle without saying a word and speed away.

Teecher shakes his head. "Now in my sister's neighborhood? What is going on out here?"

Teecher turns to see his sister, a middle-aged woman in a bright yellow dress, standing where Mr. Turner was just lying.

"What is going on out here?" his sister asks looking around.

"It was nothing Rhonda, some people looking for a new place." Teecher ushers her back into her home, a large estate on one of the most prestigious areas of the Empire.

"Well, I am waiting for Mr. Turner," Rhonda exclaims. "He is bringing me some of the best bulbs from his flower garden this year."

Teecher pushes her toward the grand doors a little harder. "He will ring the bell when he arrives my dear."

"I guess so," she answers as she looks out for Mr. Turner one last time before going into her home.

Teecher looks as well before going in and shutting the door behind them.

"I am going to finish dinner in the kitchen," Rhonda tells him before yelling, "Sam! Your uncle is here!"

Teecher smiles at her. "Old fashioned way to get him down here."

"Darn right," she says as she disappears into the kitchen.

"T-T!" a tiny voice calls out. "T-T!"

Teecher's usually grim face turns slightly warm. "I am here my boy!"

From around the corner the owner of the tiny voice appears, a boy that anyone would say fit his minute vocal performance, a mouse of a child with sandy brown hair, huge eye glasses, and freckles caked onto his dark face.

Upon seeing Teecher, he lets out the same syllables once again. "T-T!"

Teecher grabs him up into a hug, warmly bellowing, "How have you been my little Sam?"

Sam thinks for a second. "Good. How about you? I saw you on TV again."

"That is getting old for you isn't it?"

Sam shakes his head no.

"No?" Teecher asks before tickling him. They both laugh together.

"Wait," Sam stops their joyful moment. "I have been wanting to talk with you about the Verse since last week."

"Oh ya," Teecher says, putting him down on the sofa to sit with him. "Learned some stuff from the Big Speak, did you?"

"Yes," Sam answers, "but I wanted to ask you about history."

"What?" Teecher peers at him. "What's that?"

"You don't know what history is?" Sam asks him.

"No," suddenly Teecher is angry. "Who told you that word?"

"Mrs. Granger at school. It means that stuff happened in the past. And learning about it."

"Well, that is what the Verse is for, to learn about our past."

Sam looks frustrated.

"Well, what is it now little one?"

Sam waits to say it. "The Verse only talks about Empire history."

"So?" Teecher eyes him.

"So what about what happened before the bomb? I mean the land or lands, what were they called? And what did we do? Were the sports different?"

Teecher laughs dismissively. "The sports?"

His uncle's answers and attitude have made Sam angry, disappointed too.

"All you need to know is right there. Before the bomb the whites were the main rulers, they were evil devils, they almost destroyed the Earth with their bombs. We were given a chance as the chosen people of Godallah through the prophet DeShawn. What else do you need to know?"

"Well, how did the whites become so powerful?" Sam quickly asks.

Teecher has no direct answer.

"I mean, did we all have a war and they won that war, like before the final war? Or were they just always the rulers?"

Teecher shakes his head. "I don't know. I mean you don't need to know these small details. Let's just say we had our areas of the world and whites who started out with the smallest continent in the world, eventually conquered all of them. Now that is more than I can tell you."

Teecher grabs Sam again for a hug.

Sam stops him. "Is it top secret information?"

Teecher smiles. "It really is."

Sam thinks about it of a second, excited by the thought of being so close to top secret stuff.

"Alright you two," Rhonda interrupts. "It is time for dinner."

Teecher's radio buzzes.

Rhonda acknowledges the call. "We will go in and wait for you."

Teecher nods. Once the room is clear he answers the call. "Yes? End."

A mechanical voice answers. "Update request on 311 from the Elder White Hunters. End."

Teecher scrunches his face in deep thought for a few moments. The radio waits in silence. Finally, "He is ready. A bit squeamish, but I will take care of that. End."

Teecher bites his lip, waiting for the reply.

At last the mechanical voice repeats, "Squeamish? End."

Teecher slams his hand on the living table in front of him. "Yes, I've seen and fixed this before. More times than you want to know. End."

The mechanical voice answers quickly, "Affirmative. End."

Teecher shoves his radio back onto his belt. "Affirmative," he says to himself as if listening to the phonemes of the word for the first time.

13

Hunter 311 and Tysheka sit at a high red booth within the famous Hunter Restaurant. Tysheka's eyes are frozen wide as she looks at the many dishes on their table.

"They are going to bring two of every dish they have on the menu," Hunter 311 informs.

"This is unreal," Tysheka exclaims. Then she turns to her uncle, "But I thought this was supposed to be some huge celebration with all the Hunters?"

Other Hunters inside the restaurant stare at Hunter 311 and Tysheka, muttering to each other. Hunter 311 attempts to ignore them.

"It is true that it has been tradition. But not all Hunters have big celebrations upon their anointment time. For instance Hunter 303 held an intimate dinner with his beloved. If you know your Hunter History."

Tysheka smacks her lips. "They made us read that in like third grade. And I am your niece, not your beloved. Leading us back to what I was saying in the car, you need a girlfriend."

"Food is getting cold!" Hunter 311 interrupts. He begins to dig into the first wave of dishes.

Tysheka shakes her head at her uncle before digging in.

After trying every dish on the table Tysheka goes on. "So can I safely say you really don't want to be a Hunter?"

Hunter 311 spits out his bite of food. "What?" He blurts out lowly as if caught doing something wrong, then looks around to see if anyone heard her comment. "Of course I do, don't talk like that."

Tysheka eyes her uncle.

Hunter 311 leans forward. "I mean, I have never been able to think about it."

Tysheka leans forward too. "Maybe you could have a hobby on the side, you know, in your spare time. Something to make you more of a Renaissance man. If you are ever going to score a woman you will need a bit of depth." She looks around at the other Hunters. "Especially compared to the average Hunter."

Hunter 311 doesn't understand. "What do you mean?"

She thinks about it. "They seem, I don't know, dull."

Hunter 311 laughs. "Oh, really?"

"Ya, like real buzz kills."

Hunter 311 scopes the Hunters in the restaurant area with them. Several, at least three are looking toward them.

"Being so important, so famous, why aren't any of them dating the who's who of the Empire?"

Hunter 311 smiles. "Like who?"

"Like some actress or singer. Like Daytrona Houston or Ebony Knowles."

Hunter laughs. "I have no idea who those people are."

"That is my point," she declares. "You are so out of touch as a Hunter."

Hunter 311 crosses his arms. "This is what I am to do in life. I have finished training and now I will serve the Empire till I die."

"You are special uncle," Tysheka continues. "What do you think you would like to do, or is there something you've found from your years in the Academy you like doing?"

Hunter 311 ponders her question hard for a good while, but alas he could not come up with any solid answer at all.

"The years at the Academy were not the greatest were they uncle?" The niece takes her uncle's hand.

"They were," Hunter 311 says, "what they were." He places his other hand onto hers now.

"I know it really screwed up mom when the Empire took you. And grandma and grandpa."

Hunter 311 looks away.

Tysheka knows it is touchy for her mother or uncle to talk about it. Her mom had commented many times that it eventually killed her parents.

Hunter 311 speaks finally. "But, I just remembered I have something on the side, a hobby if you will, already."

Tysheka smiles. "Nice change the subject move, since," she pulls one hand away, "I would really like to find something for you to do on the side or you may just end up like," she presents the Hunters behind her, "this."

Hunter 311 laughs.

"So," she asks. "What is it?"

"Well, for a few years now I have been involved with the agricultural projects at the Academy."

Tysheka's nose curls up. "Like with that fruit and veggie guy Gardner?"

"Yes, he is a friend. We have worked on some very important projects." Her uncle goes on, "And I really love it. I am also really good at it. I mean I produced the best harvests in the history of the school."

"I've been seeing him in the news lately with all those new fruits they are producing now. I was wondering, why doesn't he have a number like the rest of the Hunters?"

"What?" Hunter asks almost as if not hearing her.

"He is called by his name, I take it his birth name."

"Oh yes," Hunter 311 understands now. "I do not know. Good question."

"So you want to grow fruit, veggies, and herbs in your spare time?"

"I have worked on all three, but I would prefer to focus on herbs. But, I would actually have to put a lot of time into it so it may not work."

"O.K. But herbs?"

Hunter 311 chuckles, slightly embarrassed. "I can grow fruits and veggies, but herbs are my passion. I can get heady nugs on an herb plant that weigh at 16 ounces when dried, indoor grown."

"Alright, besides the fact I have no idea what you are talking about, what would you do with the herbs, heal people, sell them to doctors?"

Hunter 311 seems to realize his niece has no knowledge of the herb. "Do you have any ideas that may be better for my hobby time?"

Tysheka thinks about it for a second. "Well, like I said, you are not the typical Hunter. Maybe you could be a figure of change."

Hunter 311 smirks at her statement. "And how could I do that?"

Tysheka thinks hard again. "Maybe as a politician? A voice of the people? A voice of reason?"

Hunter 311 shakes his head at her before checking the other Hunter's attentions once again. Two sets of staring Hunters are now gone. But now only one group of three remains in the corner, staring at Hunter 311 at that moment.

"And you my niece," Hunter 311 takes a drink of wine, "should be a comedian."

14

The men in white rubber suits strap Mr. Turner to a shiny mental gurney and wheel him down a bleached white hallway.

Mr. Turner mumbles incoherently, but a few understandable words emanate from his old lips. "Lies, lies. Whites and lies."

The older man in white turns to his co-worker. "Isn't this?"

"Yes," the other man in white blurts, attempting to quiet the older, yet seemingly more immature worker.

"He is the Engineer," the older man in white says in astonishment.

"Yes, now help me with him," the younger man in white unstraps Mr. Turner.

The older man opens a large metal door with a small frosted window. Inside is a metal seat, the entire interior scorched black.

The two plop Mr. Turner into the metal chair and quickly slam the door shut.

The older man pulls a level to the right of the door. Bright fire engulfs the room and Mr. Turner.

"And now all his secrets die with him," the younger man utters.

III

The Anointed

1

Above the planet Earth, North America seems to be almost divided in half by a huge body of water running from the Great Lakes to the Gulf of Mexico. The only significant light source emanates from the Colored Empire.

Far below, Teecher and Hunter 311 drive along a trail-like road in the Western wilderness. The inside of the vehicle is bare-bones, over painted in white and blue, with rust showing through underneath the paint. The heaping mass of metal pieces, created long ago in a factory that has long been rubble, roars along with new life through a rebuilt engine.

"I can still remember being 5-years old at the Academy," Hunter 311 tells his Teecher. "The bulletin came over the screens saying whites had been spotted after 100 years."

Teecher looks over at his new protégé. "And look at you now. On the Hunt."

"Well, at the time I thought the world was ending," Hunter 311 admits. "Thoughts of war and hordes of whites flooded my mind."

"You should give thanks that such a thing did not happen," Teecher says, looks at the young Hunter. "Your generation would of never made it during the Cleansing. Smart whites were everywhere when we first came up."

Teecher hits the brakes hard, stopping from full speed into a dusty skid. He turns to his subordinate and barks, "Turn on the radar and log in Hunter 311."

Hunter 311 does as he is told.

Teecher activates his infrared sights on the dash and scans the horizon.

"Was there a report of a white?" Hunter 311 asks studying his teacher. "I didn't hear anything on the radio."

Teecher moves to checking the mirrors. "We need no report of a sighting. We are always on patrol for whites, hence the title White Hunter."

Hunter 311 smacks his lips silently. "The occurrence of a white is—"

Teecher interrupts, "Silence!" Teecher orders Hunter 311 as he stares straight ahead.

Hunter 311 uncomfortably shifts in his seat. "Finding a white on a Hunter's anointment is even rarer, isn't it?"

"We found one on your last training assignment didn't we?" Teecher points out.

Hunter 311 nods, thinking about it once again.

Teecher continues to focus his attention forward for a few moments. Finally, he turns to his student. "So the real lessons begin here." He pushes a button on the vehicle console and a screen rises. Teecher continues, "What I am about to tell you is highly classified. Do you understand?"

Hunter 311 sits upright in his seat now. "Of course, sir."

Teecher nods before going on, "Whites are not as rare as the public believes or is let to know. There actually has been a rise in their appearances as of late."

Hunter 311's eyes widen. "Appearances?"

Teecher pushes a button again, footage begins playing on the screen. The first frame shows the words "government secret" upon the emblem of the Colored Empire. Then the screen shows countless mug shots of whites, all with long unkempt hair.

"These are the whites we have found since that day when you were 5-years old," Teecher states.

The screen begins playing footage clips of each capture. The first was a lone white male, crazed and confused. His body barely covered with crude animal hide.

"They began showing up that year," Teecher says. "The only thing is that they kept coming."

Hunter 311 is amazed.

The screen shows the next white, another man very similar looking to the first.

"Each sighting was mostly lone individuals, more likely to be male," Teecher adds.

The screen shows a woman capture. The woman has similar attire, wild hair.

"How often do they show up?" Hunter 311 asks.

"After the first came, more followed, and our best statisticians could only come up with one reliable pattern."

"What?" Hunter 311 wants to know.

"That sightings have become exponentially increased each year." Teecher looks at Hunter 311 seriously. "That pattern stays true to this day."

Hunter 311 gulps in fear as he thinks.

Teecher pulls a pair of binoculars from a compartment near the floor and peers through them at the horizon. "Yes, in the last few months there has been a high percentage of them spotted in this very vicinity."

Hunter 311 begins to look around now. "How many whites do you think there is out there still?"

Teecher shakes his head still peering into the binoculars. "We may never know my young Hunter."

The young Hunter keeps up his queries. "How do you know there has been more sightings?"

Teecher pulls the binoculars from his eyes, annoyed, and snaps, "How do I know? I've had to pop more of them lately than I've had to in years! As soon as they come up I find 'em and sacrifice 'em to Godallah! And that's all you should care about too! Especially with what you just found out, haven't you learned that if anything?"

Hunter 311 repeats Teecher's words, "Come up? And where do you think they come from when you spot them?"

Teecher puts the binoculars down and faces Hunter 311 now. "They come up from the ground. It is a theory conceived by our best scientists." Teecher begins peering into the binoculars once again.

Hunter 311 searches the distance from his side window. He whispers lowly to himself, "They come up from the ground just as we did."

Teecher's keen ears hear him clearly. "What?" He grabs Hunter 311 by the collar, dropping the binoculars. "These savages are nothing like us! I don't ever want to hear that comparison again, got it?"

"Yes, I got it," Hunter 311 speaks, fear in his eyes.

Teecher lets him go and sit back in his seat. "If thinking about the thrill of the Hunt doesn't suit your stomach, then perhaps you should be thinking about positive things in your life now that you have your freedom. Like spending time with that little niece you always talk about."

Hunter 311 smiles with the thought of her. "I will get to see her a lot more." He reaches in his jacket pocket and reveals a picture of a little girl. The caption reads, "To uncle, from Tysheka."

"You know," Hunter 311 informs Teecher. "I had my ceremonial banquet with her at the Hunter's Restaurant last night?"

Teecher is disgusted. He eyes Hunter 311. "I talked to you about your banquet several times."

"I know," Hunter 311 interjects. "I just wanted something small with my family."

"And I explained the necessity of the banquet as a blessed entrance into the White Hunter faction!" Teecher goes on. "The Hunters wait for years for a banquet. The others at the restaurant must have been outraged!"

Hunter 311 shrugs. "The chef was glad he only had to make two of everything on the menu, instead making one of everything for each Hunter."

Teecher shakes his head and grunts loudly. "He is supposed to make one of everything for each Hunter!"

"I know that is tradition," Hunter 311 lowers his head.

Teecher watches the new Hunter out of the corner of his eye. "Just do me one favor," he asks. "Just be the best Hunter you can be."

Hunter gives a quick nod. "Of course. You know I was thinking of taking on a dog. Maybe that would help me do just that."

"Depends on the dog really," Teecher answers. "A pit bull is the abomination of the dog. It has no use for a Hunter. It cannot track well. It will not let go of its bite in battle."

Hunter 311 frowns. "It won't?"

"Yes. The pit-bull is far too common in the Empire, almost becoming rampant." Teecher contends. "Why, over the years I have had to kill more of the stupid mongrels when they've attacked citizens than I've killed whites."

Hunter 311 just listens.

Teecher sees his young protégé is unconvinced. "But, I'll tell you a little history I know about the dog. The pit bull was one of many breeds of dog that existed before the war. Even though your generation only knows the pit-bull, several breeds came down originally with our forefathers."

Hunter 311 inquires, "Other breeds?"

Teecher goes on, "The pit bull is only one form of the dog. Other breeds look different, height, weight, form, hair, and so forth."

Hunter 311 begins to imagine. "I wonder what they looked like."

Teecher looks out through his binoculars again. "The only description I ever heard was a breed that died out underground because only two were taken. They were larger than pits, all short hair, black with brown markings on their muzzle, chest and legs. Their ears stood straight up like a bat. Their muzzle was long like a wolf. Supposedly, as smart as a human."

Hunter 311 imagines his teacher's description. "Now that's a dog, right?

"Damn right," Teecher replies.

Hunter 311 looks out his window again. The horizon ends not far away as if they are near a ridge. He looks back at Teacher, "What will my life be like besides hunting?"

Teecher shrugs. "Now you have your own apartment and don't have to live with the other pupils anymore, you can actually have a life."

Hunter 311 ponders the possibilities for a moment. Time with his sister, niece, sight-seeing in the city, eating at the cafe on Malcolm X Boulevard.

Teecher interrupts his thoughts. "My first memory of going to my Hunter apartment was the garden inside." He laughs, puts his binoculars down. "I'd never grown my food before. You take for granted the Academy's three square meals."

Hunter 311 is worried now. "I have to grow my own food?"

Teecher laughs again and slaps Hunter 311 on the shoulder. "See? These are the issues you should be thinking about. Not frustrating yourself by trying to figure out these savages." Teecher puts the car in drive. It slowly rolls over each hill of the trail like a ship on the waves of the sea. The surrounding grass suddenly gets even taller around them.

Both men scan the horizon.

Teecher eyes the radar in his pupil's hands. "So what do you see?"

Hunter 311 studies the grass line outside his window. "What do I see? Nothing. This grass would provide anyone hiding in it with thick cover."

"The radar Hunter! What do you see on the radar?"

Hunter 311 jumps, dropping the radar on the floorboard.

Teecher shakes his head.

Hunter 311 grabs the radar from the floor and scrambles to keep it in his hands. Once he regains control he studies the screen. "Nothing, Teecher."

Teecher begins chewing on his lip. He reveals a bottle from a compartment in the car and takes a swig. "Many times in life it looks as if there is nothing there. When really, something is there staring you right in the face." He puts the flask away then yells, "Come on!" Suddenly, Teecher jumps from the car and dashes into the tall grass.

Pupil 311 watches for a second, unmoved, but snaps out of it and springs from the car to follow Teecher.

Teecher sprints like a professional athlete over the grassy hills, seeming to have a specific direction. He transcends hill after hill in a second each.

Pupil 311 attempts to follow him, pumping his legs into the fastest run he possibly can. Just when he thinks he may never catch up, Teecher stops suddenly and Hunter 311 almost runs into him.

The young Hunter pants, "What did you see Teecher?"

Teecher peers out into the grass before him. "Now that you are about to be anointed I might as well tell you. After your life training you are supposed to have much greater breath."

Hunter 311 is hurt by the negative comment. "I've never had the stamina my classmates have."

Teecher snarls, "And for that reason you need to be the most ferocious Hunter in the league!"

Suddenly, the giant teacher dashes to the nearby hillside and rips an elderly white man hiding in the grass. He drags the old man back and throws him down before Hunter 311. "You need not hunt the first kill my ex-pupil. And in your case I feel this method would be best."

2

An unknown observer peers from a dark enclosure through a small opening. Inside the darkness the figure wears a name tag with "Ritchie" printed on it.

From Ritchie's view, Teecher, Hunter 311, and the old white man are only a stone's throw away.

3

Hunter 311 surveys the white man. He wears more clothes than the man Teecher eliminated earlier wore. He is aged to at least sixty, long gray hair and beard.

He speaks the same unfamiliar tongue. "Preeze yall. Preeze!"

Hunter 311 is again frozen.

The old white man continues his babble. "Preeze! Preeze!"

Hunter 311 listens carefully. "What is he saying?"

Teecher looks at the old man with hatred. He kicks him in the mouth and screams, "Shut up old man!" Blood gushes from the man's mouth.

Hunter 311 blurts, "I think he just said please!"

Teecher is furious now. He points at his student. "You shut up too!"

Hunter 311 is horrified.

Teecher grabs the old man by his hair and drags him to Hunter 311's side. "Since you were given to me a year ago, as tradition dictates, I have come to the conclusion you are weak. You do not have the conviction to kill."

Teecher draws his giant Bowie knife from a hidden sheath in his pants and offers it to the new Hunter. "You may have been bestowed with a new name. But you will never be a true Hunter unless you sanctify this position in blood right now."

4

The hidden spy named Ritchie watches on. The area he is hiding in is blended perfectly within the surrounding tall grass. The tiny opening he is peering from is practically undetectable from afar.

Ritchie zooms in on Teecher. The red record circle blinks in the corner of his screen.

"Not another one," Ritchie utters through his gritted teeth.

5

    Hunter 311 does not take the knife, just stares at it.
    Teecher shakes his head at him. "That's what I thought."
    The white old man watches his two captors from below not knowing what they are talking about.
    Teecher retracts the blade from his offer to his student. "So," he states, "there is a solution my latest pupil." Teecher hands the knife to the old man.
    The old man keeps completely still, not understanding.
    Quickly frustrated, Teecher now shoves the handle of the knife to him and the old man takes it and leaps up.
    "What?" the young Hunter stammers, "What are you doing Teecher?"
    The old man stands before Teecher and Hunter 311 holding the giant knife out, still trembling, his entire chin caked with blood.
    Teecher looks in the old man's eyes, then points to Hunter 311.
    The young Hunter cannot believe what he is seeing. "Teecher! No! Why?"
    The old man seems baffled, still doesn't move.
    Teecher now makes stabbing motions and points at Hunter 311 again. Then he pulls out his pistol and points it at the old man.
    The old man recognizes a gun, his eyes widen with fear.
    Teecher points at Hunter 311 once again.
    The white old man understands. He lets out a wild shriek and tackles Hunter 311 as he tries to plunge the knife into the young Hunter's chest.
    Teecher bellows with sinister laughter.
    Hunter 311 struggles and holds the knife at bay. Sweat pours from his brow as the two push against each other with all their might.

"Stop," Hunter 311 grunts a plea to the old man, "I think you said please."

The white old man still puts on pressure, but seems to think about what Hunter 311 has said. He looks up at Teecher.

Teecher wags his pistol at his side as a reminder.

The old man looks back at the young Hunter with a look of desperation before he continues his onslaught again. He tries a final shove, but Hunter 311 turns the blade at the last second, impaling him from below. Blood oozes all over the young Hunter, and the white old man slumps on top of him.

Teecher laughs hardily.

IV

The Butterfly

1

At first Ritchie seems to be dazed from what he just witnessed. Then he swings a keyboard in front of him and begins rapidly typing.

2

Hunter 311 pushes the old man's dead body off of him and screams, "Why did you do that?" The young Hunter springs to his feet, rushing his ex-teacher with a war cry, "Answer me!"

Teecher eagerly awaits him.

Hunter 311 grabs Teecher by the collar, getting right in his face and again screaming. "Why?"

Teecher still doesn't move, smiles calmly and asks, "You done? Got it all out?"

Hunter 311 grips his teacher's collar harder, begins to raise his right arm.

In an instant Teecher flips Hunter 311 on his head. Before the young Hunter can react he is swung around onto his back. Teecher easily holds him down with a one-hand choke while his other is raised and ready to strike.

Teecher screams at him, "You see? You are no Hunter. No warrior. And I have signed my name on you!"

Hunter 311 tries to squirm and cower away. Teecher holds him still.

"That's why you are going to do what I say and change your ways during your probationary period with me! "Teecher steps up and lifts the young dazed Hunter to his feet by his collar. "But let me tell you, if you don't change, or if you touch me again, I will kill you and leave your body out here for the wild animals to eat, understand?"

Hunter 311 nods, frozen with fear.

Teecher lets go of Hunter 311's collar with a push.

3

Inside the dark enclosure Ritchie watches the two Hunters walk away from the bloody scene. Their figures go over the first hill, then the second.

He looks at his screen, stops the video recording, and saves the file among many others in a folder named "Killings."

4

Teecher gets back into the driver's seat of the Hunter vehicle.

Hunter 311 throws up atop a nearby hill. After he stands right outside his door. His face has become ashen and dazed.

Teecher calls out to the young Hunter, "See what I mean? You're in shock for Godallah's sake."

Hunter 311 stares at nothing.

Teecher shakes his head at his student. He yells loudly at him, "Hunter 311! Come on already!"

Hunter 311 tries to say something, but his muscles won't agree with his thoughts. Teecher screams at him. "Hunter 311!"

The age-old 311 part of his name snaps him out of it. Hunter 311 shakes his head. "Yes, yes sir." He enters the vehicle and sits down, notices the blood on his shirt. "Blood," he states lowly.

"Yes, blood," Teecher replies. "Your anointed blood. Be proud." Teecher shakes his head at him. "Somehow."

Hunter 311 is bewildered. "I'm anointed?"

Teecher does not look at his latest Hunter as he speaks. "Yes, how does it feel?"

Hunter 311 thinks, then feels like he is about to be sick. He gathers himself mentally by thinking of Tysheka, but stays silent.

Teecher goes on. "It will pass." He looks over at Hunter 311. "I hope."

Hunter 311 begins to breathe now, almost for the first time in minutes.

Teecher looks at the horizon in front of them, then the mirrors. "You need to know there may be more out here. Some are dangerous Hunter 311."

Hunter 311 snaps his head towards Teecher. "More?"

5

From Ritchie's view he can see the Hunter vehicle. He turns on an old rusty device next to him. Fuzz blares in his headset. Ritchie turns a dial until Teecher and Hunter's voice come in clear.

Hunter 311's voice is tiny, a squeaking tone. "So how many whites have you killed?" Teecher's voice is thunder in comparison. "In my whole life? Too many to remember."

There is a silence for a few beats.

6

Hunter 311 clutches his stomach. He begins to speak, "I think I'm going," but stops abruptly. His eyes are fixed on the horizon. "Teecher," he gasps out, "I see something in the grass."

7

Ritchie reaches up inside the enclosure to swing a mechanical arm to his right eye. In the periscope-like device Ritchie sees an even greater optical zoom view of Hunter 311 now in the vehicle.

Hunter 311 stares right at him and his location.

"Shit," Ritchie blurts out.

Hunter 311 points in the direction of Ritchie's hidden location. His voice squeaks through Ritchie's headset. "I think I see movement and something flashing red!"

8

"Where?" Teecher asks scanning the grassy horizon in the same direction with his binoculars. The only motion is the grass swaying in the wind.

"It was just right there," Hunter 311 contends.

Just then Teecher seems to see something. He frantically turns on the ignition and revs the engine. Without looking he begins flipping a series of switches.

Two large guns rise from the Hunter vehicle hood with a hum.

Hunter 311 is staggered. "Guns in the hood?"

"Watch the horizon!" Teecher orders.

Hunter 311 whips his attention back to the area, suddenly, a bush within the grass they are watching moves several feet. "What in the?"

Teecher turns the wheel hard and punches the Hunter vehicle, sending the car toward the movement. The moving bush remains still, despite the oncoming Hunter car.

Hunter 311 watches and cannot believe what he sees as the leaves rustle and Ritchie's head pops from the top of the mass of vegetation. He smiles and directly below his face a huge Gatling gun emerges from the bush.

Both Teecher and Hunter 311 spot Ritchie and his huge gun instantly. Hunter 311 is frozen, mouth wide open. Teecher is so stunned he hits the brakes, leaving the car skidding to a halt directly in front of Ritchie.

Ritchie's bush begins to make revving noises.

"What are we doing?" Hunter 311 pleads with Teecher.

In a blur Ritchie's moving bush torpedoes toward the Hunter vehicle, gun a blazing. Teecher has already spun the car around 180 degrees in a full on retreat before a single bullet reaches them. Yet, two hit the bumper of the Hunter vehicle right away.

Hunter 311 looks behind him, trying to get more glimpses of Ritchie. "What is it?"

"What a stupid question!" Teecher states loudly.

Ritchie pursues the two Hunters over the grassy hills, the two vehicles smashing their ways through tall grass and into the unknown.

Hunter 311 notices that the high speeds have caused much of the grass to fall from Ritchie's vehicle, revealing a metal frame and side panels.

"It is a camouflaged vehicle!" Hunter 311 shouts.

With a whine, a rocket propelled grenade launcher rises from the top of the Ritchie's vehicle.

"Another gun!" Hunter 311 yells.

Ritchie shifts gears as he gains on the Hunters. He types a code into the keyboard of his complicated dash. The sound of a turbo charger working in overdrive is heard and suddenly the vehicle picks up speed.

"He's gaining on us!" Hunter 311 screams.

The guns on Ritchie's vehicle begin to spin again, sending bullets flying toward the Hunter's car. More bullets hit the Hunter vehicle.

"Oh dump!" Hunter 311 drops down while his Teecher keeps driving.

"Hide you coward!" Teecher yells at him.

"What do you want me to do besides what I am doing right now?" Hunter 311 yells up at his Teecher.

There is a sudden explosion right outside of the passenger side of the car.

"What in Deshawn's name was that?" Hunter 311 asks from the floorboard. He looks up into his side mirror and sees smoke rising from the RPG cannon atop Ritchie's vehicle.

Teecher studies the weapon for a second in his mirror. "Technology," he answers.

Another rocket shoots from the huge barrel.

Teecher begins performing S-formations to avoid Ritchie's the projectile explosions.

Hunter 311 is frantic. "What do we do?"

Teecher jerks the wheel again. "Get on the radio!" he yells. "Brigade Captain may be near!"

Hunter 311 fumbles for the radio during the commotion. Once turned on, the speaker crackles. He pushes the button on the radio and yells into the receiver. "Hunter 311 here! We need help! End."

Brigade Captain's voice suddenly booms over the speaker. "Rookie! Congratulations! Have a problem already? End."

Teecher jerks the wheel again to avoid another rocket.

Hunter 311 pushes the button again. "A white is chasing us! End." Hunter 311 waits for a reply. Silence. "Did you copy?"

Finally the voice booms over the radio again. "Chasing you? End."

Hunter eagerly replies. "Yes! And shooting bursts of fire at us! End."

Another silence. The Captain's voice returns sooner this time. "Is this a joke? Did Teecher put you up to this?"

Hunter 311 goes on frantically. "This is not a joke, there is—"

Teecher grabs the radio from Hunter 311. "Listen Captain! We have a class one detection! Do you read? Class one detection! End."

Brigade Captain responds quickly. "No. Are you sure?"

Suddenly another rocket skims the side of the vehicle, creating a loud blast into the radio. Teecher pushes the button to speak again. "There is no question!" Teecher jerks the wheel again. "If I don't see you again, tell the council to begin the plan! Out." Teecher throws the radio to the floor.

Hunter 311 looks to his teacher. "What is the plan?"

Teecher veers to the right suddenly. "Look, no more questions. If we survive this, I'll answer any question you have, alright?"

Hunter 311 nods. "Yes, sir."

The two cars are very close to each other now. Yet, Ritchie has stopped firing both of his weapons. He is so close now the front of his vehicle almost touches the bumper of the Hunter vehicle.

Ritchie speeds up and gets on the side of the Hunters, smiling at them, then slows to get behind the Hunter vehicle again. Once behind them, Ritchie begins to fire again.

Teecher continues to concentrate on swerving from possible rockets and bullets.

The rolling hills stretch out into the horizon before them. The blue sky meets a final hill and drops abruptly into a large ravine.

Atop the crest of the a hill Hunter 311 spots the drop off. "Teecher, a canyon!"

Teecher seems to ignore the young Hunter, saying nothing.

The two vehicles close in on the last hill. In the last spilt second, Hunter 311 leaps from his car door right before the car leaves the ground and plummets into the canyon below. Hunter 311 rolls onto the grass, hitting his head on a rock and losing consciousness.

Ritchie's vehicle does a quick U-turn right before its departure into the ravine. It stops suddenly, the partially grass-covered door opens and Ritchie steps out.

Hunter 311 lays on his back. The wind blows through his hair. A zebra striped butterfly lands on his lip. Ritchie's foot scares away the butterfly and gently pries at Hunter 311's mouth with the tip of his boot.

V

The Debate

1

The night floats above the Colored Empire like a dark dank blanket, covering the city, the wasteland to the West, and the Mississippi River to the East. A distant glimpse of the vanishing sun can be seen flying away in its natural Westward journey.

The river bed stretches out vastly in width, now more than ten times as wide as it once was. Its water now runs impure, animals and plants that must devour it still obtain radioactive effects that can kill and mutate.

A rather short wall divides the city from the wasteland and the river. Like veins of a complex organism, this wall also lines the endless array of buildings and architectural wonders from different eras of the city. The wall branches through the city, passing Romanesque buildings and monuments, extravagant houses, crude structures built during a poorer economic times, apartments, and even charred remnants of buildings that lasted the Final War.

The once filled main walkway that runs through the entire city is now empty. Four main buildings lie in the center of the city in a cross formation. The temple lies to the East.

One of the tallest structures in the city is a charred and dilapidated skyscraper to the West. The building reads "Hunter Academy" in huge engraved letters. But if you look closely and understand the long forgotten written language, you can make out a sign saying, "Westin Peachtree Plaza."

The King's castle, a more intact skyscraper with an antenna, rests to the North. A huge plaque hangs above the entrance reading, "The only large building built before the war that still stands only because the protection of Godallah. The Castle of the King of the Colored Empire: 55 floors."

A rotunda lies South, a huge white structure with giant pillars on all sides. The building sits on a hill and has its own engraving reading, "Georgia State Built Politic Hill: A True Democracy for the Colored Empire."

Inside the Politic Hill building the five Head White Hunters end their conversation and open the giant oak door before them. The men are large, older, and wear a similar style uniform as Teecher, but with more colors on their breasts. They all have a serious look on their faces. The Head White Hunters enter a vast hall filled with men and women in pews. Upon seeing the men, many of the room's occupants applaud and cheer.

Each pew seat has a small screen and a keypad with the words "Voter Pad" in bright yellow printed above them. Huge television screens line the walls of the vast room.

The Head White Hunters climb to fill in their positions at the stage of cascading desks set at the focal point of the great hall. Applause continues as the elder Hunters wave to the audience before sitting in the top row of seats. The door opposite of the one the Head White Hunters entered from opens and five other men enter. A great applause roars through the hall once again, though this cheer is dissimilar from the cheering for the Hunters. These cheers seem more conservative somehow, pointing to their source as a different group or class than the first. The cheers are for the Senators of the Colored Empire.

These five Senators look quite different than the Head White Hunters, most are even older, smaller men, the aura of intelligence and patience in them. They saunter to their respective seats while the Head White Hunters look on, a few openly impatient.

The applause ends much sooner than the Head White Hunter's as well. The hall falls silent, edgy, and a few in the back still talk amongst each other. The old men wave to the crowd before taking their seats below the Head White Hunters.

A man in a tuxedo emerges with a microphone. He is pristine, in a crisp dark suit and looks, almost as if he was a human cut out. A light blares over him suddenly, illuminating his bright skin and sharp features. A camera drops from the ceiling and settles perfectly in front of him.

His everlasting razor smile begins to generate a television show host voice. "Hello everyone! I'm the Man with the Microphone and it is debate time in our Politic Hill again! I hope everyone at home is ready to partake in your sacred duty to watch and Vote! Wait for the Vote sign to light up and do your duty! Don't forget folks we have the first true democracy in history!"

The audience cheers loudly.

2

An average family of citizens is gathered around a kitchen television watching the debate. All have their Voter-Pads in hand, even small children.

The family's 10-year old boy, Demetrious, switches his attention from his Voter-Pad to the family's front door. "Come on Tysheka," he whispers to himself.

Just then the door opens and Tysheka comes in. The other family members do not even notice her as she enters, the door shutting behind her.

"You almost missed the beginning," Demetrious says as he greets her with the standard Empire handshake.

"You know I don't really care about Voting," Tysheka waves the event off.

Demetrious looks around, paranoid who is listening. "You know you cannot talk like that around here, Ty."

Tysheka rolls her eyes.

"Come on," Demetrious puts his hand on her shoulder. "Let's just go watch the Debate in the boy's room."

The two leave the main living and kitchen combination room and follow a short back hall to three doors. Demetrious opens the door to their left and they enter the room.

"It's a boy's room alright," Tysheka comments as she notices the mess.

Demetrious kicks some clothes and other items off the couch and motions for her to sit. He doesn't notice that Tysheka finishes cleaning the area before sitting.

"It's starting!" Demetrious cries as the Debate begins playing on his huge screen.

Tysheka rolls her eyes again.

3

A local giant bar holds hundreds of citizens watching the Debate, all holding their handheld Voter Pads or sitting in front of Voter Pads built into the bar and tables.

Cicily and Crsytal exit the girl's bathroom. The club is so packed she can barely get back to her table. After squeezing through countless people they finally spot Monique.

"Oh my Godallah," Cicily complains. "I smell like a horde of clubbers now."

Crystal laughs. "We just literally were forced to rub against a horde of clubbers so it stands to reason."

Monique chimes in. "But doesn't it turn you on?"

Cicily sits down at their table. "You've been horny since I met you in high school."

"Yeah, maybe you have a hormone disorder Monique," Crystal adds. The group laughs.

The screens in the bar start ringing.

"It's starting!" someone in the bar screams.

Everyone shuts up and gets their Voter-Pads ready.

"What is going on?" Crystal asks another bar patron.

"There has been an Emergency Debate called!" the patron answers excitedly.

"I wonder why?" Cicily asks aloud.

4

An older man in a tank top sits in his old recliner chair rooting for the Debate. A tiny table over his lap holds his economically sized meal of fruits and veges and his prized Voter-Pad.

5

Broadcasting from Politic Hill, the Man with the Microphone boogies for a second, then halts and speaks. "Alright! As the Colored system goes: we have the Hunters against the Senators folks! And don't forget this date ladies and gentlemen, because this is the third ever Emergency Debate! That's right: An Emergency Debate! I can barely remember being a wee young cat when the second ED occurred!" The man with the microphone pulls out his handkerchief and wipes his forehead. "Whoa people!"

The Debate attendants rise and cheer. The entire building shakes.

The man with microphone goes on. "Since this Debate has been called by the Head White Hunters, noble Lieutenant Hunter will hold the floor first!"

A good portion of the attendants leap to their feet and scream for the Lieutenant as he rises. The leader of the Head White Hunters is a giant old man with long white dreadlocks and beard. Yet, his facial hair is not like the white savages, instead it is neatly cut and braided. His time in service shows as even his giant breast barely possesses enough room for the numerous medals pinned upon it. His voice is ageless, deep, and powerful. "Hello, my people. It is my duty to call this Debate for a serious reason. It seems we have a problem we have never encountered before or planned for."

The audience does not cheer for the first time.

The Lieutenant Hunter proceeds. "First, let me begin by going over a bit of history for the people. I have been involved in countless Debates over the past 20 years. Each resulted in blockading every single proposal to fund any type of army or protection of our city! And thus these last two decades my elite force of White Hunters have merely policed areas outside the city."

The other head Hunters grunt in agreement.

The Lieutenant Hunter stands still and silent for a moment as he ponders the consequences of what he is about to say. Finally, he goes on, "There is only one way to say this: Over the years my force has encountered more whites than the people have been led to believe."

The crowd goes in an uproar, boos, cries of fear ring through the hall.

The Lieutenant Hunter raises his hand to call for order. "I understand many of your feelings about this deception. But I can assure you the deception was something the White Hunters were against."

The Head White Hunters scowl down at the old men below them.

The Lieutenant Hunter continues. "Two important facts need to be known by the people, the Voters, before my time is up. One, the amount of whites we have encountered since coming up is not the figure we live with everyday, not the number 14 as is posted in every house, business, and street within our great city."

The Lieutenant Hunter spies the Debate clock running out of time. He begins again, speaking more rapidly. "The actual numbers are now at 232, many savages like the ones the people have seen. But more importantly," the Lieutenant Hunter spits out as the last two seconds run out, "an intelligent, violent, and technologically savvy white has been spotted."

"What?" the man with microphone cuts in. "Time's up for Lieutenant Hunter!"

All the people in attendance gasp at the news, many throw boos and swear words.

6

The older man in the recliner spits his bite of food out upon hearing the Lieutenant Hunter's last Debate statement.

7

"What the hell is going on?" Crystal asks.

"I don't know," Monique answers, eyes still frozen on the nearest Debate screen.

Cicily is the only person in the entire bar not looking at a screen. She looks down and utters, "My brother just became a Hunter."

"Oh no," Monique says, "He could die!"

"Shut up!" Crystal orders Monique. Then she turns to Cicily. "Don't worry Cicily, your brother has been training since he was five. He can take care of himself."

"Oh my Godallah," Monique says. "I totally forgot they took your little brother when he was five years old. I mean, how old were you?"

"Shut up!" both Crystal and Cicily order Crystal.

8

Demetrious is very excited. "To think! A smart white man! A warrior!" He begins to imagine it. "An evil warrior, with powers from the evil side! The light side! The white side!"

Tysheka ignores him. She is pondering the dangers her uncle, a new-found Hunter, will now face. "What is going on? And what will happen to my uncle?" she thinks to herself.

"Hey," Demetrious blurts, poking Tysheka's shoulder. "Are you hearing this?"

"Yes!" Tysheka answers angrily. "It is not cool."

"Not cool? It's the coolest!" Demetrious turns to her excited, but her look jolts his memory and he realizes. "Oh yeah, your uncle has just become a Hunter, so you're afraid he will be in danger."

"You figured it out," Tysheka says sarcastically. "A genius."

Demetrious eyes her. "What is it with you lately?"

"What?" She looks away with disinterest.

"The last couple of months you've been so different. And now you are writing some biographical novel? Are you going to get it published?"

"It's not a novel moron. It's more like," she thinks for a second, "a diary."

"Just get your Pad ready," Demetrious tells her. "Voting will start any second."

9

Inside Politic Hill, the Vote Sign lights up and people instantly begin typing away on their Voter-Pads.

10

The old man in the recliner throws his plate of food against his living room wall and begins typing madly into his Voter-Pad.

11

The average family of citizens each bow their heads to punch their Votes into their Voter-Pads.

In the other room, Demetrious punches his Vote in his Voter-Pad excitedly. Then he looks over at Tysheka. She stills still, Voter-Pad in her lap, not Voting.

"What are you doing?" Demetrious almost yells.

Tysheka snaps out of it. "Oh," she says, picking her Voter-Pad up and punching in her Vote.

12

    Every bar patron and employee stop their conversation or work to give themselves to the Voting Ritual.
    Cicily, Crystal, and Monique concentrate as they punch their Votes in.

13

Inside the Politic Hill the Lieutenant Hunter sits again.

The Man with the Microphone leaps into the air, landing in a dance pose. He holds the microphone to his mouth and sings, "Elder Senator Mathis is recognized!"

The head Senator is a plump old man with tiny spectacles and top hat. He seems scared of the unruly crowd. He clears his throat slightly and begins to speak. "Now, now folks. Please calm down."

More boos.

"As usual," Senator Mathis debates. "Our dedicated Hunters' take on most things is extreme. From the information I have received there is only one sophisticated white and there is a question of how technologically advanced his weapons capabilities are."

The Lieutenant Hunter interrupts the Senator. "The man was driving a bush at over 100 miles per hour while shooting rocket propelled grenades at two Hunters!"

The audience roars in terror!

The Man with Microphone slides forward for a close up. "Lieutenant Hunter interrupts and that could cost him! Will the Voters deduct a point from his score?"

The Vote Light comes on and the Empire does its duty.

The Senator waits for the Vote to end and tries to qualm the spectators by waving his hands downward.

"Or," the Man with the Microphone articulates, "Will Senator's inability to control the audience be his downfall?"

Senator Mathis continues. "Empirical studies which have been conducted in those 20-years the Lieutenant is referring to show no evidence to spend such sizeable amounts of money for more weapons or individual soldiers. After all, such money should be used in the way of the Colored System, for living expenses and festivals, and making our lives the best they can be. Preparing for a fantastic tale of an invading white army with technology beyond our own? The idea is scientifically unfounded blasphemy!"

The people in the many pews boo loudly.

The Vote light is activated and the people choose their number.

"The sighting of one relatively intelligent white by no means proves that he is from an empire." Senator Mathis sees his time is running out. "Whites creating an empire like ours! The Extermination cleansed the devils from the Earth!"

The Man with Microphone steps in again. "Time is up for Senator Mathis!"

14

"He makes sense," Monique makes a point, "We waste our money for nothing and life could just suck!"

"You are so stupid," Crystal tells Monique. "All you think about is partying and sex!"

"Honestly, what else is there?" Monique retorts.

No answer from anyone.

"Well, the man's argument includes the Bible," Monique responds.

"Funny point coming from you," Crystal snickers. "You can't even remember his name, or that he is a Senator even."

Monique shrugs.

Cicely remains silent.

15

"This guy is a coward!" Demetrious shouts at the screen. He turns to Tysheka and whispers, "You shouldn't Vote for him."

She ignores him, holding on tight to her Voter-Pad.

"Here it comes," Demetrious says in anticipation of Vote time.

16

The Vote Sign lights up in Politic Hill. The people cheer and everyone Votes.

17

"You fear monger!" Demetrious punches his Vote against Mathis into his Voter-Pad.

For very different reasons, Tysheka punches in the same Vote.

18

The bar is loud even during Voting.
The three girls Vote and then look at each other with worry.

19

The camera shoots to the Man with the Microphone. "Next time slot goes to Head White Hunter Sergeant Hunter."

The Sergeant is a shorter, younger man. His face is clean shaven and his hair is trimmed more than the other Hunters. He rises and speaks. "I have been one of Lieutenant Hunter's biggest supporters. With this event, I have no doubt that this is the beginning of the end of our Empire if we do not rally forces now."

The audience screams in offense to the Head White Hunter's comment.

The Vote Light turns on and the people punch away at their keypads.

Sergeant Hunter waits for the Vote to end and quickly backs up his first statement. "Now you know I love our people. That is why we need to act quickly. This man is just the first of what will become many more!"

The citizens' faces in the audience grow with fear.

The Sergeant goes on. "The Great Wars and Extermination may have merely eradicated white civilizations near our Empire, but I believe there are other areas on our planet that humans are capable of living. Why has the theory of a possible white civilization been deemed fantasy, legend, and blasphemy? They have always been savages. And savages are dangerous!"

Some of the audience cheers.

Sergeant Hunter finishes. "The law states, they will conquer. It is evil that has made this possible. It is not blasphemy to prepare against evil! I am ending my time."

The Sergeant sits down.

The Man with the Microphone goes to one knee. "Sergeant Hunter retains his extra time for his next session!"

20

"Sergeant! Sergeant!" Demetrious chants as he dances in front of the couch. He has put on his Hunter costume.

Tysheka rolls her eyes at him again.

21

"He's scaring me," Monique whines to her friends.

Cicily puts her arm around Monique. "It's going to be alright," she assures her.

The Vote Sign lights up on the screens across the bar.

"Let's just Vote," Crystal says.

22

The Man with the Microphone announces, "Up next is the Empire's greatest scientist, Senator Harlow Williams! We heard about 20-years of studies in the past, possibly areas in the world which are habitable other than our own, but what will a current scientific view of this situation be? Let's find out!"

The greatest scientist may be the smallest citizen. His head barely makes it to his microphone. He starts to speak, but cannot be heard. Senator Mathis reaches over and lowers the microphone for him.

"Thank you Senator," Senator Williams begins. "Thank you citizens of the Colored Empire. I have come here today to speak in the language I always have. It is the language of empiricism, of observation, and of parsimony."

The audience does not cheer, instead they seem to try a figure out what the Senator is saying. "Now let us take this event into consideration of a complete picture according to what we have observed before," the Senator scientist speaks softly into the microphone. "First, we have a recent positive sighting of one white with weapons technology. Second, we have exterminated, admittingly and regrettably without providing this fact to the public awareness, hundreds of whites without the capabilities of higher thinking for many years. Third, we have never once observed a sign of another civilization outside the Empire at all, let alone a white civilization. What does this tell us?"

The audience waits for the answer.

"It tells us my good citizens," Senator Williams answers, "that this man is alone, a freak of nature, the most reasonable explanation is he is the last of a people that dwelled underground just as our people have."

The audience seems to agree.

Senator Williams sees the audience liking where he is going, but does not waste time, goes on. "But the important part of the theory is that we can eliminate one fairly easy as compared to more. We merely need to rally and reinforce the current White Hunter squad." The scientist Senator's points make the audience cheer loudly. The Man with the Microphone jumps up and down. "Time is up for the greatest scientist on Earth! If he says it folks, I believe it!"

23

"Sounds like a bunch of gibberish to me," Monique comments.

"This time I agree," Crystal says. "I hate people who do nothing but memorize really long words so they can use them in conversations with people and look smart. They suck bad."

"He is merely using the most simple solutions and theories to back the Senator's agenda," Cicily speaks out.

Her best friends are impressed. "Where did that come from?" Monique asks.

Before Cicily can answer the Vote Light goes on. Everyone punches their Votes into their Voter-Pads.

24

Demetrious is appalled as he punches in his Vote. "Stinking nerd!" He turns to Tysheka. "I cannot believe his, so-called, logic!"

25

The Man with the Microphone is on the screen once again. "Now we have a special treat for you all tonight!" He raises his free arm in introduction, his other arm stays in its everlasting position, always within the microphone's pickup range of his voice. "Next up is Brigade Captain, a special witness called by the Elder Hunters!"

A curtain in the background opens and a rap band begins to play. The audience claps and grooves in their seats.

The Man with the Microphone introduces the band. "Give a hand for NeezeyLife's band of the month: The Womanizers!"

"The leader of the band raps into his headset. "Important things: Gettin' Paid, Gettin' Laid, and I introduce to you the Captain of the White Hunter Brigade!"

The doors open and Brigade Captain enters the hall. The people in the hall pews rise and cheer for the active Hunter. The Hunter stops before the Senators and Head White Hunters, a microphone lowers before him.

Brigade Captain steps up to the microphone and clears his throat. "Hello all." He pauses, show a sign of uncertainty before beginning again. "I was in the field today and took the transmission from the two Hunters who encountered the intelligent white. I have the recording of what transpired, it is short, but is graphic. You folks may want to have the children leave the room."

The Man with the Microphone steps in again. "But remember folks, a true Vote comes only from those citizens who know true facts. Children or not."

The audience oohs and awes.

The Man with the Microphone points to the ceiling and shouts, "Go!"

The sound of a recording beginning is played throughout the hall. First comes the squeak of Hunter 311, "Hunter 311 here! We need help!"

26

Cicily's eyes widen in terror as she utters, "That is my brother!"

27

A murmur echoes within Politic Hill until the transmission continues. Brigade Captain's voice answers, "Rookie! Congratulations! What is the problem already?"

Hunter 311 speaks again. "A white is chasing us!"

The audience reacts with fear and shock to the last comment.

"Chasing you?" Brigade Captain replies.

"Yes!" Hunter 311. "And shooting bursts of fire at us!"

Gasps and cries from the crowd.

Brigade Captain's sarcastic tone, "Is this a joke? Did your teacher-"

Hunter 311 snaps, "This is not a joke, there is-"

A muffled sound is heard throughout the hall. Spectators look at each with wonder. Then another voice comes over the speakers. It is Teecher. "Brigade Captain listen. We have the problem we thought we never would. A class one evolution!"

The Captain's voice waivers. "No. Are you serious?"

Teecher's voice becomes low now, but still very serious. "If I don't see you again, tell Politic Hill they must pass the measure! Out."

The spectators lose it. Voters cry, clutching their Voter Pads and their hearts.

After a quick consult Senator Mathis stands. "Objection! The recording clearly stated political direction!"

The Man with the Microphone does another dance. "An objection from Senator Mathis! You know the rules folks!" the Man with the Microphone yells. "Proceedings cannot go on without the gears of our Empire doing their work." The Man with the Microphone looks into the camera. "And that is you folks! Does the objection stand? You decide!"

The Vote Sign lights up. The audience seems especially excited to Vote.

"What," the Man with the Microphone asks the Empire, "will the outcome be?"

28

"Vote no!" Cicily screams as she Votes. "Vote no to the objection everyone!" She turns to her friends. "I have to hear the rest of that transmission. I need to know what happened to my brother!"

Her friends nod seriously. Crystal says, "You can count on us Cill." They punch their Votes into the Voter-Pads.

29

"Awesome!" Demetrious punches his Vote against the objection. Then he turns to Tysheka, "Can you believe it?"

Tysheka is gone.

Demetrious looks around. "Tysheka?" he calls out to an empty room.

30

The Man with the Microphone turns to the giant screen behind him for the result. Suddenly, the screen flashes an X.

"And the motion of objection has been shot down!" the Man with the Microphone exclaims.

The audience generates its habitual roar.

"Proceed," the Man with the Microphone declares, signaling Brigade Captain to go on.

The Hunter gives a sad expression before continuing. "The point is this white killed one of the greatest Hunters in history today."

The audience roars with terror.

Brigade Captain shouts, "The Hunter known as Teecher was killed today."

Teecher's picture appears on the screens around the Empire.

Brigade Captain keeps up his voice. "Presumably the newly anointed Hunter 311 is dead as well, yet initial scientific observations of what is left of the vehicle show the passenger door may have been opened before final impact."

Hunter 311's picture now replaces Teecher's.

"The tragedy of the century!" the Man with the Microphone announces as he looks up at the young Hunter's photo on the giant screen above him.

Cameras shoot back to Brigade Captain, who gives the audience and the viewers one last serious look before stating lowly, "That's all I have." He then saunters away from the microphone and sits down in an empty chair in the front row of the audience.

The Man with the Microphone steps forward into camera view. "Thank you Captain for that most rare testimony and audio recording of today's terrorist attack. We appreciate the sacrifices you make in the line of duty." The Man with the

Microphone turns to the camera. "I mean what in DeShawn's Name is happening? You Voters will decide."

The Vote Sign lights up.

Even the Man with the Microphone begins to Vote on camera. He quickly slips his high tech Vote Pad into his breast pocket. "Sorry folks. Camera 1 here was supposed to be pointed elsewhere," he says lowly into the camera before raising his voice in an announcement "And now: The Senator from the North Senator Cedric Makin!"

The brightest man in the hall stands. Senator Cedric Makin is dressed luxuriously. Donned from head to toe in the color purple, a suede dob hat with a tall feather, suit, and boots in rich royal purple. Senator Makin clears his throat with a loud grunt before beginning to speak. "In what context can we create an army? Do we even know how? Our citizen's have no skills in combat! An army would need a draft and for those of you who do not know what that is: A draft is when a great number of the young male citizens would be forced to be in the army and train to fight away from your family and loved ones, against their will!"

The audience screams profanity at the idea.

"Yes, I agree!" Senator Makin yells. "That is what these Hunters are proposing. These are obviously valiant men, yet their courage stems from lifelong training! We mere citizens being forced into such a lifestyle all of a sudden would have drastic consequences! Not to mention the inefficiency that the resulting army would have!"

Many spectators scream in approval and agreement.

"All we know is self sufficiency! You know the way," Senator Makin points to the audience and then the camera. "Each citizen grows his own food, takes care of his own, families band together. The only people in the entire Empire who have a cause, a job if you will, are the Hunters. We cannot make an army, at least not immediately." He signals the end of his time by saying, "I am sitting now."

Many spectators scream in pleasure again, others boo.

31

"A draft sounds like it would suck," Monique says to her friends. "I mean there would be way less guys, right?"

"Please," Crystal asks again. "Shut up."

Monique rolls her eyes and looks away.

Monique looks to Cicily. "Are you alright Cill?"

Cicily answers with a nod. She waits for the Vote Light on the screen.

32

The giant Vote Light in Politic Hill begins to burn bright and every Colored citizen types a number on their Voter-Pads.

The camera switches back to the Man with Microphone. "Senator Cedric Makin sits. Whether it is to save time for later debates, or did the Senator's send Makin's short and sweet argument in at the end to keep his points fresh for the final Vote? For the truth, we have to wait and see! We have run the cycle! The debate is over! Boy those Senators know how to play the game, sending Senator Makin, a true game closer, in at the end like that!"

The screens make a whining buzz suddenly.

"Results are in Colored Empire!" The Man with the Microphone retrieves his Voter-Pad and reads something on its screen. "Yes! It looks like some records have been broken here tonight!"

The scores pop up on the screens throughout the hall.

The Man with the Microphone points to the largest screen behind him. "And Senator Makin has broken a scoring record for his session! Yes, a 27 overall and 9 deep folks!"

Many spectators in the hall scream with approval, others look as if they could kill.

The Head White Hunters are very displeased.

33

The kitchen of the average Colored home celebrate by dancing together.

Demetrious looks at them with animosity from the hall. "I hate my family so much," he utters to himself.

34

Inside the vast bar many citizens and workers dance or clap with joy for the result of the debate. Drinks flow and confetti floats around the giant room.

Except the three girls. Cicily sits and cries, her friends surround her for comfort.

35

The old man jumps from his tattered recliner chair, sending his lap tray and Voter-Pad flying. He waves his hand in disgust at the screen.

36

Pupil 315 peers out the dormitory window. He pushes a button and the glass slides open. The orange heat flows into the large room.

"Hey! What are you doing?" Hunter 316 rises from a community table.

"None of your business!" Pupil 315 snaps at him.

The young Pupil 316 backs down.

But, Pupil 315 answers. "Can't you hear that?"

Everyone listens. All the citizens of the Empire scream.

"What is that?" Pupil 317 asks.

"I heard one of the Hunters say there was an Emergency Debate today," Pupil 315 peers down into the city and tries to listen. "Something happened. And people are not happy."

"Why don't they let us watch the Debate?" Pupil 318 asks.

"Because we will never Vote," his twin bother answers him. Pupil 317 flicks his 316 badge. "I wasn't asking you."

"Then who were you asking?" The young 5-year old Pupil 318 pops up next to 316.

"Him," Pupil 317 points to Pupil 315 at the window.

Pupil 315 pushes the button to close the window and looks back. "It's because they are hiding something from us."

37

The King's skyscraper seems to jut from the city ground like a large tarnished tooth among a mouth full of rotten and missing teeth. In the highest level the King's throne room lies in an old board room of a one-time Fortune 500 company.

Treasures found after the Colored People came back out from the ground decorate the room. A hybrid form of hip-hop plays on huge speakers.

At the back of the long room is the supreme leader of the land, King Amses. He sits upon his reclining throne, drinking Hennessey from the bottle. He is a young, lanky man dressed in gold ceremonial garb and sunglasses.

A jester dances in front of him. He begins to rap, but the King waves him away. The music stops.

King Amses studies his bottle. "I wish you could find more of this stuff."

The head adviser to the King, Harold, stands off to the side, but quickly slinks up to the throne. "We can try, my King," Harold rasps. "Yet, it is highly unlikely. The bottle was found in the Earth outside the city walls. As you know, such finds are rare."

The King huffs. "Well, perhaps we should put some money into digs out there. Who knows what you could bring me?"

"Yes, my King," Harold says bowing.

A ring is heard and the final vote is automatically displayed on King Amses' huge television screen.

The King ignores it, instead taking a bite of fried chicken and another swig of his rare bottle. Everyone in the throne room reads the topic and results on the screen, desperately wanting to speak to each other, yet being forced to silence in front of the King.

Finally, Harold speaks. "My King, I wanted to know if I could direct your attention to the results of the Debate."

The King waves his hand toward the screen without looking at it. "Yes, I know. I noticed you and the servants sneaking around with your little Voterpads. I really don't care either way. It's the same every time they meet. More money for festivals and monotony. No change."

Harold gives a round of looks to his coworkers, who have nothing. He gulps, sweating. "My King, you should look at the screen for yourself. There is a change I'm afraid."

King Amses is in shock. "What?" The King turns toward his television and reads. The screen reads, "Today's Debate topic: Intelligent white with technologically advanced weapons has been spotted, killed the legendary Teecher, and captured or killed the new Hunter 311. Should funds go into an army to protect the city from any outside attack? Vote result: Senators vote no - 54 and Hunters vote yes - 40."

The King almost falls from his throne. He rises and immediately proceeds out the door with no instructions. His entourage give each other a grimace only for an instant before swarming behind him.

Harold reaches his King first, asking him. "My King, where are you going?"

King Amses marches forward without even giving a look to his advisor. "Why to intervene of course!"

38

Outside the Empire walls the entire fleet of Hunters await orders in their vehicles.

Brigade Captain stands with his car door open as he listens to a voice over the radio. His pit-bull awaits action in the passenger seat.

"I have those coordinates. Out." Brigade Captain puts the radio back on his belt and steps up on the floorboard of his vehicle. "We are heading West!" he screams to the fleet before ducking into his cruiser and taking off.

The Hunters eagerly race after.

VI

The Truth

1

Hunter 311 awakens in a pitch black. He looks around, frozen with fear. A white hand lights a match. The young Hunter faces away from his captor, comes to fully realize what has happened, and instead twists around to face the light source.

Ritchie stands there with a smile and lit match. He is dressed in jeans, flannel, and leather jacket.

Hunter 311 scurries backwards and away from Ritchie like a fearful animal.

Ritchie begins to light the lanterns bolted to the cave wall as Hunter 311 remains immobile in a corner, his eyes watching Ritchie all the while. "I brought you here for a reason," Ritchie speaks.

Hunter 311 is astounded to hear a white speak English. "You speak our language?"

Ritchie lights another lantern, the room gets brighter. "My language too. Everyone spoke it in this country."

Hunter 311 is confused. "Country?"

Ritchie smiles. "Yeah, it was called the United States of America."

"How do you know that?" Hunter 311 asks.

"I am a history buff." He lights another lamp. "But what I really want to talk about is your people's history."

Hunter 311 doesn't seem to understand where this is going. "All there is, is the Bible Wall and the Law."

Ritchie nods with a hint of sarcasm. "I've been doing a little reading myself. The Great Wars, the Extermination."

Hunter 311 is suddenly uneasy. "You have?"

"Yes, colorful history you all have." He stares at Hunter 311. "Or lack of color I should say."

Hunter 311 shifts his weight and tries to look away. "Well, that was a long time ago," he says.

Ritchie catches his eyes, "But not much change in all that time."

Silence for a few moments. Then Hunter 311 shakes his head and mutters, "No."

"The weird thing about this world is that the history we learn is not always what happened," Ritchie says as he lights another lantern.

Hunter 311 scowls. "What do you mean?"

"Don't get me wrong, the color of blood is all over your civilization's hands, from the Great Wars and Extermination, or whatever you call it, to what you are still doing now," Ritchie goes on as he lights another lantern. "That's what I brought you here for," he says. "To show you something."

Hunter 311 is interested. "What?" he asks, attention still set on Ritchie.

Ritchie lights a final wall lamp and turns to him. "The Bible Wall."

Hunter 311 is confused and offended. "I saw the Bible Wall for the first time today for your information."

Ritchie begins to walk backward into the darkness. "Not all of it."

Hunter 311 keeps his expression going. "What do you mean not all of it?"

Ritchie disappears from Hunter 311's view for a moment. Then he lights the final lantern making the room they are in completely lit up.

Hunter 311 looks around in the light finally and beholds where they are, his eyes widen with realization. He looks around now. "We are in the cave of the Bible Wall!"

"Not quite," Ritchie says, "Look closely."

Hunter 311 sees now that they are not in the cave his Teecher took him earlier, but in an obvious connection to it. There is a giant mural on the cave wall drawn in the same fashion as the other murals, upon closer examination the rookie Hunter discovers the mural has been cut off by packed stone.

"It's a continuation of the Bible Wall in the Temple!" Hunter 311 exclaims lowly.

"This is the final message of your Bible," Ritchie states.

Hunter 311 stares at the murals, amazed, but still confused. "What message?"

"Can't you tell?" Ritchie asks.

Hunter 311 examines the mural. It depicts a huge mass of people marching toward the sun. The group is something Hunter 311 has never seen before. There are men, women, children, young and old, except one thing is clearly not right to him. The people are an eclectic mass of whites, blacks, and every race in between.

Ritchie gets closer to Hunter 311 now. "It's something wonderful that once existed in this world."

"Wonderful?" Hunter 311 whispers, "What was it?"

Ritchie gazes over Hunter 311's shoulder at the mural. "It is unity," he answers, "It is peace, tolerance, and acceptance."

The young White Hunter has no idea what Ritchie is saying. Although perfect English in the 20th century, these words are foreign to a citizen of the Colored Empire.

Hunter 311 gets close to inspect the mural better. "There's all types of different colored people, not just black and white! Yellow, tan, red!"

Ritchie puts his arm around Hunter 311. "Yeah, isn't it beautiful?"

Hunter 311 is still in shock. He finally notices Ritchie's arm around him, and politely slips away. "Yes," Hunter 311 answers, "But, where are these people?"

Ritchie seems slightly solemn. "I don't know. Maybe they died during your Empire's past conflicts. Maybe they are in other parts of the world." He thinks about his own family, all gone now. "I want to find out."

Hunter 311 ponders for a second as well, then focuses on the bottom of the mural.

The letters NAACP are painted in white.

Hunter 311 crouches before the letters, traces them with his finger. "What does NAACP mean?"

"It stands for the National Association for the Advancement of Colored People," Ritchie answers. "It's the organization that funded your bunker."

Hunter 311 looks back to Ritchie. "Bunker?"

"The underground cave your people lived in," Ritchie says.

Hunter 311 looks at the letters again. "That makes sense, we still call ourselves Colored."

Ritchie crouches next to Hunter 311. "But what doesn't make sense is who the NAACP was. I had to look the letters up in the archive to find out."

"Archives?" Hunter 311 asks.

Ritchie rises. "Yes, information about the history of the world before the war."

"What did they say about NAACP?" Hunter 311 asks.

Ritchie stands before the mural peering up at it. "According to the archives, the NAACP stood for the advancement of colored people, but also for the unity of all peoples." Ritchie points at the mural. "The Colored race had a history of oppression in the United States of America so the NAACP was created to help them be equal in society."

"Where did these archives come from?" Hunter 311 asks. "How do we know the information in them are real?"

"It is information that was available to the world before the war," Ritchie explains, "Information collected, kept, and added to by my family."

"Your family?" Hunter 311 is worried suddenly, thoughts of the barbarians, the explosions during the chase.

Ritchie smiles, almost wallowing in his fear. "Yes, my family, but don't worry, I am the last of my kind." The smile fades. "For months I have searched this area, between the river and the wasteland, for others like me, like my family. The occasions I witnessed anyone with my skin color, they were like the ones your Hunters killed, possessing very low intelligence or some sort of dementia."

"I don't know what demen-chia is," Hunter 311 tries to pronounce the word, "But low intelligence is right. You are the first white my people have witnessed that has any form of higher intelligence at all for hundreds of years."

"I would agree," Ritchie says. "Each time I witnessed one they seemed to have no language, although I was unsure as they were all killed by one of your Hunters before I could investigate further."

"That is what we do," Hunter 311 utters. "But somehow I never realized."

Ritchie frowns at Hunter 311, but the frown is abruptly replaced with a look of determination. "Look," he says to Hunter 311. Ritchie turns to the rookie Hunter. "It seems like your people twisted that set of values into the insane culture you now have." He points at the formed rock dividing the final mural from the Colored Empire's sacred cave. "And they hide that fact from their people."

Hunter 311 is in shock as he thinks about what this means, his entire life, childhood in the training facility, dissociation from family.

Ritchie stands right in front of Hunter 311, staring directly in his eyes. "I saw your so-called anointment. I saw what your teacher did to you. I've watched these Hunters kill helpless men over and over since I came to the surface. You did not want to kill that man, and in fact the kill was in self-defense thanks to your very respectable teacher."

Hunter 311 wants space, ashamed.

"Don't feel bad man!" Ritchie grabs his shoulder for a moment. "You are not like them. You are a good person. That's why I didn't kill you!"

Hunter 311 snaps at him. "But why make up such a lie?"

Ritchie shrugs. "Maybe fear turned into hate when faced with something or someone different from themselves. Especially after all those years down here with nothing but themselves."

Hunter 311 thinks about it, a tear drops from his eye. But, suddenly an idea comes to his mind. "You know of the history of our," he tries to sound out the new word, "cun-ter-ee?"

Ritchie nods.

"My descendants took much information down with them. Computer memory made it easier for them to attempt to retain the history of the world."

Hunter 311 ponders in amazement for a few seconds. New possibilities that he never knew existed begin to enter his mind. "Tell me why it all happened?"

"All what?" Ritchie asks.

"The war," Hunter 311 answers. "Was it the whites that caused it?"

Ritchie laughs. "Shit no! The United States of America was a melting pot of many races and cultures all living together. The war was caused by radical religious groups gaining access to atomic weapons."

"Atomic?" Hunter 311 repeats.

Ritchie's eyebrows pop up, "Big, big, big boom."

"I understand," Hunter 311 says.

Both look down for a moment.

"So how did your people survive?" Hunter 311 asks.

"Funny story." Ritchie laughs again. "I am descended from several families that built a bunker not too far from your NAACP bunker. They went down with as much as they could when the war began. Already had a self-sufficient garden and other food sources."

Ritchie motions to the cave they are in. "A little nicer than this I'm afraid."

Hunter 311 gives him a dismissing wave. "The metal used in what you refer to as the bunker has long been taken out. Only a cave remains."

"Really?" Ritchie exclaims, "I never would of guessed." He studies the cavern by running his white hand over the cave wall and ceiling.

Hunter 311 has a thought. "The people in your bunker were all white?"

"Hell no," Ritchie sniggers. "There were many races, ethnicities, and religions."

"What happened to all of them?" Hunter 311 asks eagerly.

"Well," Ritchie says. "Eventually the procreation just wasn't going to happen, no matter the need for humanity to survive. After so many generations, people were too interrelated to marry or just picky." Ritchie kicks a stone. "In the end it was my mother and I. When she died I stayed down for a good while. She always told me the nuclear fallout was long gone by now and I could go up. Finally, I did." Ritchie gives a hard look at Hunter 311. "Too bad what I found when I came up was a place where I was hunted for the color of my skin."

2

"Have you seen 312, 313, or 314?" Pupil 315 asks as he reenters the dormitory.

The other Pupils look up from their activities with no information.

"They weren't at dinner," Pupil 315 looks out the window. "They never came back from their one on ones."

"Maybe they went out with their big brothers!" little Pupil 318 exclaims.

"That is not possible," Pupil 316 corrects him. "Pupils are not to go out with any Hunter until the three month processing period before graduation."

"Yet, that must be where they are," Pupil 315 concludes.

"Have you ever seen that before?" Pupil 316 asks him.

"No, never." Pupil 315 answers. He feels like smashing through the window.

3

Tysheka is more relieved the further she is from Demetrious' house. She stops only for a second to check her watch before going on again.

She heads into a city park and sits beneath a large old oak tree. Revealing a tape recorder, she pushes the red button on it, sets the device next to her and begins to speak.

"Until recently, she was openly content with life. But in the last few months strange and new feelings and thoughts were overwhelming her. The Debate and Demetrious were just too much for her and she yearned to be away from the stress and worry of her life, though meaningless it was in the end and regards to the grand scheme of things.

For instance, she had always felt an unexplainable awkwardness surrounding her culture, the ways of the Empire. Her mother, and many mother's lack of responsibility, the government's push for recreational activities, the lack of father's in Empire homes. All of this never sat well with her and she was asking questions about where daddy and momma was at an early age to her relatives and teachers.

Even her mother seemed to share this trait. And despite these feelings, her mother would attempt ever so desperately to fit right in with societal expectations regarding behavior, almost always out with her girlfriends at some bar or club.

And now her uncle may be gone forever. How did this fit into her realization about the world and herself? Would it merely lead to the eventual conclusion that life is solely a fleeting mishap of short but tangible moments that always add up to nothing for a googolplex of individuals desperately trying to deal with their inevitable mortalities, all on a rock floating a billion miles an hour in space.

She had been thinking about all of this for some time, and only recently had come to something of a conclusion if you will.

So it was upon realizing this conclusion that she began searching for alternative ways of feeling better. And like she told herself, perhaps it was all in a search to find the reason for life.

Unfortunately, in the Empire there was a limited amount of things to make one feel better or even capture one's attention for any significant amount of time. Most drank, smoked, gathered at social spots if there was not one of many government funded holidays going on.

She first thought of her father, searching for him, but soon found the Empire had established a system that made it next to impossible to find out paternity of a child.

So she set out to find something that captured her heart, that she could complete over and over with passion, a hobby, a trade, something to take up time, but prove valuable as well. And she felt after eight days of searching, she must find this hobby, this passion today.

If my uncle can find herbs, I can find something, she tells herself out loud as she walks toward the deadly wastelands."

Tysheka pushes the red button again and stares out into the peaceful green scenery.

"Care to comment on the recent events and Debate?" a woman's voice calls out near her.

Before Tysheka can react, a reporter appears out of nowhere and ambushes her, three crew men behind her. The woman shoves a microphone in her face and one of the men points a bulky camera at her.

"Have a comment for Empire News?" the reporter asks again, her fake smile frozen in an upward position.

"No, no I don't," Tysheka answers, putting her hand up.

One of the crewmen points at her, "That's Tysheka Washington! Hunter 311's niece!" he shouts to the reporter.

The female reporter's eyes widen, she instantly perks up and pounces. "Care to comment on how you are feeling now that your uncle has gone missing and is presumed dead?"

Tysheka grabs her belongings and quickly rises, rushing away from them.

"Do you know where Hunter 311 is?" the reporter yells as she flees.

"What do you think of this supposedly technologically advanced white?" the reporter keeps asking as if automation.

"Please Ms. Washington, just one comment!"

4

Several miles West of the Colored Empire's city limits the White Hunter fleet speed toward the coordinates.

Brigade Captain gets on his radio. "We're 30 minutes till ETA, sir. Out." He replaces the radio and signals forward to the fleet with his hand.

5

"We are sitting ducks," Cicily slurs. "You saw what one of them did? Just think of several, or an army was to come through here?"

Bar patrons begin to listen to her.

"My brother has been trained since he was a toddler to fight, and look at what one did to him and his experienced Teecher?"

"I think you should be quiet," Monique says.

"Shut up bitch," Cicily gives her a look of seriousness.

Monique steps back in fear.

Cicily takes another shot.

"You should slow down though, girlfriend," Crystal advises.

"Be quiet. Slow down," Cicily mimics her the two girls. Then, with all the intent of detaching from Monique, if not from Crystal as well, she scans the bar for another source of social interaction.

"What are you doing?" Crystal asks her drunk friend.

"None of your business." Cicily continues to look around until she finds what she has been looking for. "Now, maybe we can meet back up in a few minutes?"

Crystal and Monique look to the man Cicily has spotted sitting alone across the bar. He is large, not too handsome, dressed well for the establishment.

Crystal makes a decision to intervene. "Not tonight, what about Tysh-"

Cicily raises her hand to her best friend's mouth. "Don't even put the mother guilt trip into this." She rises from her bar stool and straightens her outfit.

"Your makeup," Monique hands Tysheka her compact.

Cicily smiles at her, takes it, and fixes the damage the crying had done. She hands it back to Monique when she is done. "I'll be quick," Cicily slurs, "Meet back in 15 minutes." She shakes herself slightly before making her way over to the man.

After Cicily is several feet away Monique quips. "What an emotion whore."

Cicily hears her, but doesn't acknowledge it physically or emotionally. She has her eyes set on the prize. He watches one of the giant stretch screens on the bar wall.

Crystal and Monique gather their belongings.

"Let's grab something from my garden for dinner," Monique proposes.

Crystal nods. "We can eat there real quick and bring something back for Cicily. Some food will help sober her up."

Monique's eyebrows raise. "That is if she wants to be sober after banging that guy."

The two girls eye Cicily approaching the man before they exit the bar.

"Hello there," Cicily purrs to the man.

He seems taken aback, looking around. "Me? Um, hello."

"I see you are sitting all alone here," Cicily looks at the open seat next to him.

"Yes?" He stares at her silently.

She begins to twirl her hair. "Are you expecting someone?"

"Me?" he says again. "No, no one."

Cicily giggles as much as she can at her age before hopping onto the chair. "Then I am sure you don't mind if I join you?"

The man smiles. "What for?"

Cicily eyes him. "I didn't take you for a such a direct man."

The man doesn't seem to follow her.

"I thought maybe we could have some fun?" She runs her finger down her chest to her bra line.

The man understands. "Well, yes," he says excitedly, "Alright, where?"

Cicily shrugs. "This place is pretty clear after the Debate, why not one of the restrooms?"

The man looks around, smiles bashfully. "Um, alright," he agrees.

Cicily hops from the stool, pleased. "Great." She walks over to her table and downs her last shot. "Let's go."

The man follows Cicily into a back restroom stall.

6

Inside Politic Hill the audience has cleared out, leaving trash and debris everywhere. The Senators and Head White Hunters remain talking among themselves.

The Head White Hunters finally get up to leave. As they near the exit, the two giant doors suddenly open, stopping them in their tracks.

Young girls swarms in and throw rose petals onto the ground before King Amses steps into the hall. His entourage follows, advisors and guards.

"Oh stop," King Amses orders as he motions the flower girls away. The Senators rise and scurry to stand before the King, but opposite of the Head White Hunters. Each elder Hunter greets the King the same, the hand straight up salute.

The Senators each bow.

"Yes, yes," King Amses says. "Quit the formals."

The King glances at both groups, looks back to his entourage. "This is what I've been seeing since I was a child."

Harold nods in agreement.

King Amses addresses both groups. "Two groups separated like a high school clique." The King laughs. His entourage and most of the Senators laugh too. The King turns his gaze solely on the Head White Hunters. "That's what I've loved about you Hunters. You don't try to kiss ass."

The Head White Hunters say nothing.

King Amses smiles. "Not even mine."

"I do," the King goes on, "want to apologize for my long absence from the Debate. I've not shown an interest in government for so long, as it is such a boring world." The King looks at the two groups. "But it seems the world has become less boring today, hasn't it?" The King waits for answers.

Everyone is silent, frozen.

"Don't worry," King Amses says. "We are going to get to the bottom of it. Awkward silences and all."

Even his advisors are clueless.

"We," the King declares, "are going to have a discussion now. You will answer my questions and I will decide if a re-Vote is in order."

Everyone is astounded. The Head White Hunters and Senators whisper among themselves.

Harold the advisor speaks up so both groups can hear. "It is his right as King to order a re-Vote with any new evidence or testimony."

Senator Mathis speaks first, "We all know that."

"Let us get started," Lieutenant Hunter chimes in.

The King smiles. "Let us."

7

Inside the secret walled-off part of the scared Temple cave, Ritchie takes some clothes from his backpack and begins to change.

"What are you doing?" Hunter 311 asks.

"I'm getting into my disguise," Ritchie answers plainly.

Hunter 311 can tell what Ritchie is dressing up to be when he spots the Hunter insignia and colors. He laughs, "The clothes are just not enough I'm afraid."

Ritchie scours his backpack again, finds what he is looking for. "That's not all I have," he says. Ritchie reveals a Hunter helmet and a brown mask.

"What is that?" Hunter 311 asks.

Ritchie slips the mask over his head, fitting it on correctly. When he looks up he is now dark brown skinned with a wide nose and a head full of black dreads. He places the White Hunter helmet on as the finishing touch. "How do I look?"

Hunter 311 is amazed. "I can't believe it! The mask looks so real!"

There is a proud look on the face of the mask.

"I made it myself", says Ritchie. "To walk around the city in. There are no police or guards in your city. As a White Hunter, no one bothers you at all."

Hunter 311 examines the fabric on Ritchie's vest. "This is real! I am not going to ask how you got this."

Ritchie gives him a guilty look. "I'm sure you can guess."

Hunter 311 shoots Ritchie a scowl. "Why are you disguising yourself anyway?" "Because, we have to go to the real Bible Cave," Ritchie answers.

"Why?" Hunter 311 pries further.

Ritchie swings the backpack over his shoulder. "I think the final piece of the puzzle is there, somewhere."

"What do you mean?" Hunter 311 asks.

"Look," Ritchie says, grabbing Hunter 311's hand in a strong handshake. "I'm going. You don't have to come. I thought you deserved to know. I mean, you are not a Hunter. You know?"

Hunter 311 does not know what to say.

Ritchie struts away into the darkness.

8

The White Hunter fleet chops through grasslands with their vehicles.

The GPS screen on Brigade Captain's dash beeps. He pulls his radio and speaks into it. "This is it!"

Every White Hunter stops and emerges from their vehicles. Brigade Captain begins to give directions, his pit bull by his side.

"308!" he points at a Hunter. "Take five others and burn that direction!" He points to another. "309, you do the same with five others that way. If any are here, we'll find them!"

Several Hunters with flamethrowers begin to shoot the tall grass.

9

"Cicily?" Crystal calls out into the bathroom stall.
No answer.
"Cil?" Crystal enters the stall now. She hears a slight sound, whimpering, crying.

Crystal opens the almost soundproof steel toilet room door to find Cicily sitting with her head between her legs, sobbing. "Cil, what's wrong? What happened?" She crouches down to check her best friend. "Did he hurt you?"

Cicily looks up with a smile, though still crying.

"Did he hurt you?" Crystal demands.

"Not in a bad way," Cicily says laughing ever so pathetically before beginning to cry again.

Crystal shakes her head. "You need to slow down."

"Is that what I need?" Cicily still looks down. "What is my life?"

Crystal doesn't know what to say.

"I mean my parents were so distant I sometimes wonder if they were ever even real. My brother as well, my first memory was him being taken from us." Cicily rises, pulls up her panties. "And my daughter? I've made so many mistakes with her, not been there so many times, there is no way I can fix that."

Crystal thinks what to say. "You know we all do it. Party, hook up with whoever."

Cicily tries to walk, but stumbles. Crystal helps her stand up and the two begin out of the stall together.

Crystal takes Cicily to one of the sinks, runs some water. "I mean Monique can call you a whore and we can tell you to slow down or whatever, but we all do it, have our kids at home or whatever."

"Well, then what is so different about me?" Cicily looks at her friend before splashing water on her face.

Crystal look as if she doesn't want to say it, but decides to anyway, saying, "I think you do this stuff in an attempt to kill the pain, hide from your true emotions. Then after it is over you show so much distress."

Cicily laughs, turns the water off. "Distress, what a word," she says as she lurches for the door.

Crystal grabs her again before she can fall and opens the door to the restroom, leading Cicily out. "Even if drinking and banging guys did kill your pain, it must only be a temporary fix," she goes on. "If you didn't bring attention to yourself about what you've done, showing your guilt, I think you would just be one of the girls."

10

Inside Politic Hill King Amses sits facing the two groups. "First, in order for me to determine if a re-Vote will take place, I need to better understand the situation, both groups' proposals. I will start by further understanding your positions through some of my own questions." The King smiles. "If I seem a little oppositional to anyone, don't forget my role in these proceedings."

Quick glances from Senators.

Harold the advisor places himself behind the King.

The King begins. "First, to the Senators. I want to understand your position against directing funds to create an army."

The Senators all sit upright in anticipation.

The King continues. "Your main reasons are that creating an army would be illogical due to the extremely low probability whites would or could amass any type of forces?"

All the Senators look at each other quickly before Senator Mathis answers, "That is correct my King."

"Thank you," the King says, "But a group nod will suffice, just so we can quickly get through your points. That is, unless you object to my understanding of your positions."

The Senators and Head White Hunters nod to the King's directions.

"OK, so the next point the Senators have against the Head White Hunters' proposal is that it would also take away from necessities such as self-sufficiency and festivals?"

The Senators all nod.

The King goes on. "And finally, you argue such a proposal would likely end up creating an inefficient army anyway?" The Senators nod again.

King Amses faces the Head White Hunters. "Well, that was easy with them, wasn't it?" The Head White Hunters do not answer.

"I will not go over your points," the King states. "I do not need you to nod. I understand your position very well. You feel today's incident is only the beginning."

"This is a sign my King!" Sargent Hunter speaks up. "A sign for us to Hunt and strike this white devil down. It is and has always been our goal to make sure whites were eliminated, never to bond together to destroy man and the world again."

The King salutes the Head White Hunters. "I honor you my soldiers. I always have shown interest in your goal!"

The Head White Hunters are shocked by the King's words. King Amses looks up dramatically and calls to the skies. "I get a warm feeling knowing you are exterminating the last surviving white beasts from this planet!"

"Amen, my King," Harold the advisor rasps. The Head White Hunters look at each other.

Lieutenant Hunter answers his King. "We get this same feeling as you do, my King." The King spies the Lieutenant. "As one of the most outspoken of the Head White Hunters, I feel I may get an honest answers from you Lieutenant. I want to ask you Head White Hunters some questions. Let's start with the one I have been wondering since I was a child."

The Lieutenant awaits the question.

"How many more do you think there are?"

The Lieutenant speaks clear and respectfully. "As I've informed you many times in our meetings, there is no proof we are close to finding the last."

"How many new areas have you scoured in the last year?" the King asks.

"Many, my King," Lieutenant Hunter replies. "The annexed region, the wild, and even the outer regions!"

King Amses' eyes narrow. "And have you ever encountered a group of them?"

"No, my King," Lieutenant Hunter replies again.

The King goes forward.

Lieutenant Hunter is disappointed by where this is going.

Oh really, the King says with his face. "No army, a troop maybe?"

The Head White Hunters shake their heads no.

And Harold chuckles.

King Amses continues his interrogation. "What are the most whites you've ever encountered together?"

Lieutenant Hunter attempts to save his case. "I feel I should let my Sargent speak on that matter as he oversees statistical analyses."

The Sargent steps forward.

King Amses gives him a nod.

Sargent Hunter clears his throat before speaking. "Well King, we've never found more than two adults together. We have found children with adults also, leaving the max at three whites found at one time."

The King laughs.

Sargent Hunter continues. "It is important to note, the encounters have steadily gone up in the last decade. Mostly concentrated in a place not far from here in the grasslands to the West."

The King waves at the lieutenant, dismissing his comment with a snicker. "When the sightings went up I accompanied some of your men on Hunts, remember? The whites they were eliminating were mindless savages! No real sense of a Hunt. Even a sheltered teenage prince couldn't see much sport in it." King Amses thinks about the experience. "But, I always understood the necessity of the goal."

"That is all we are arguing for," Lieutenant Hunter jumps in. "And the preparation of our Empire for possible attack by more whites like this one."

Suddenly King Amses looks at him with anger and hisses, "My point is that you Head White Hunters seem more interested in a baseless theory than in the goal you are supposed to be concentrated on! A baseless theory that outright blasphemes the word of Godallah and the teachings of DeShawn!"

All present show their own type of fear or submissiveness to the angry King.

Silence.

The King adds, "And further I agree with the Senator's point that the existence of one intelligent white doesn't point to a theory of an army of them!"

The Head White Hunters seem to know where this is leading.

One that has yet to speak today moves forward slowly. He is the oldest of the Head White Hunters, Deputy Hunter.

Everyone, including the King, watch him and wait for him to speak.

The Deputy's age is heard in his rough voice. "As a vital part of this city's security for over 50-years, my King, I can only pose one question to you."

Now the King waits.

Just when the Deputy sees his King becoming impatient, he says it. "Where do they come from? If they cannot sustain themselves because of their savagery, then how do they keep coming?"

King Amses bows to the Deputy slightly. "Good day Deputy. My answer, I'm afraid is another question: Have you not investigated to where these whites are coming?"

The Head White Hunters seem to be getting tired of the King's circular reasoning.

"We've pinpointed an area, my King," Deputy Hunter replies. "Found a few short tunnels leading to dead ends."

"So you are wanting to find all the mindless beasts together at once to kill all the birds with one stone?" the King asks with an almost evil grin.

"Well," the Deputy utters, "If we could."

King Amses nods.

Harold approaches the King, the two whisper secretively to each other for a moment before Harold returns to where he was standing.

"I," the King begins, "understand your view as well Deputy Hunter. Yet, I want to reveal to you highly top secret information that likely is connected to this matter."

All are listening intently.

"We have had similar acts of terrorism before."

The Head White Hunters are shocked.

"Terrorism, my King?" Deputy asks.

The King turns his hands over. "Yes. It is more logical that this sighting was actually one of us, with a mask on."

"Who would do such a thing, my King?" Lieutenant Hunter asks, "I've never heard of such a thing in my life!"

King Amses sticks his chest out. "I've dealt with some danger myself! Why, you didn't think I stayed in the castle all day getting high and having sex with hundreds of women did you?

Everyone is silent.

King Amses gives the punch line. "Not all day I don't."

The King's entourage laughs, Harold hisses the loudest.

"But seriously," the King continues. "My father first informed me of a group which existed within the Colored Empire, a terrorist group formed some 50-years ago now, the White Hand. This group functioned by dressing up like whites and attacking people and groups of people throughout the city."

All present are shocked by this news.

"Every incident was covered up completely. Never knew how my father would do that so well. And such attacks have not occurred since his death. So the question may be: is this the same group, the White Hand, or a new group or individual?"

The two groups whisper and mumble to each other.

"So," King Amses silences them with his words, "I hope the Head White Hunters can appreciate the result of today's emergency debate and concentrate their efforts on this new information. Now that you know today's attack could be an inside job, you are in a better position to discover what is going on. I will continue to monitor the progress of this situation."

King Amses turns, marches through the doors opened by the guards, Harold and his entourage following.

The two groups begin to talk amongst themselves.

"By the way," King Amses pops his head back through the doors, silencing everyone once again. "I am sure you understand, but I am required to say it aloud. There will be no re-Vote." The King slips his head back through the doors before his guards close them.

11

"Just get on the other side of her and help me with her, that way we can get to the train much quicker!" Crystal orders Monique.

Monique huffs before becoming Cicily's left side crutch. Together the three begin to travel much faster.

"I need to sit down," Cicily mutters.

"Are you going to throw up again?" Monique quells.

"Mom?" Tysheka's voice suddenly emanates from behind the women.

The three freeze as if caught stealing.

"Yes?" Cicily responds, trying to sound upstanding and normal. She is still facing away and being held up by her two friends.

Tysheka waits for her mom and her friends to face her. "What are you doing? What is going on?"

Cicily motions for her friends to turn her around and they all three hobble in a circle until they are facing Tysheka.

"We are making our way to the train station to go have a late dinner at Crystal's place," Cicily tells her daughter.

Tysheka eyes all three women. "Why are they carrying you? Did you get hurt?"

Cicily lets out an artificial laugh. "Of course not. Just a little ill suddenly. That's all."

The four females stand there awkwardly for a few moments.

"Well," Crystal says finally, "We are going to miss that train if we do not get going."

"Yes," says Cicily. She smiles at Tysheka. "I will see you at home soon."

Tysheka rolls her eye solemnly. "Sure," she says before turning away and heading toward home.

Cicily watches her for a moment.

"She seems different lately," Crystal comments.

Cicily nods, still watching her daughter walk away from her.

"Let's go," Monique complains.

"Oh, hold on," Crystal snaps at her. She looks at Cicily, "You ready?"

Cicily nods, eyes on her little girl as she disappears around the corner. "Yes, let's go," she answers finally.

The three women begin toward the station again.

Monique smacks her lips, "Still don't know why you care what she thinks so much anyway. You the momma. I would of told my girl exactly what I was doing, I mean–"

"Shut up!" both Crystal and Cicily simultaneously silence Monique.

12

Screams are heard from somewhere in the tall grass. Several whites have been found and pinned in by a dozen Hunters.

It is a family perhaps, parents, children. They huddle together in fear as pit bulls snap at them.

A White Hunter oversees their capture and talks into his radio. "We got some! Some of the youngest adults we've ever seen!"

Brigade Captain's voice comes over the radio. "No old ones?"

"No," the White Hunter says, "the adults are not old."

"Any sign of one of them being smart?" the Captain asks him.

The Hunter studies the barbaric group. They are dirty, almost crazed looking. "I don't think so sir."

"What about our missing rookie?" Brigade Captain's voice questions.

"No sir," the Hunter answers. He looks back at the group of whites. "What should we do with these?"

Brigade Captain's voice booms back, "What do you think Hunter? Your job!"

The White Hunter holsters his radio. "Hunter 310," he calls out, "Burn them!"

The White Hunters begin to ignite their flamethrowers.

13

Tysheka enters her apartment, the door automatically opening and closing behind her. She goes to her tiny side room and turns on her music player. Loud futuristic music belts from the hidden speakers in the walls.

The bass and treble in the song shake the entire room.

14

Ritchie enters the sacred temple cave dressed in his Hunter disguise. "Come on kid," he whispers behind him.

Hunter 311 sticks his head through the doorway, checking the area before entering. The real White Hunter darts into the huge room, paranoid, but propelled by curiosity. "Why can't you just tell me what you are looking for?" he pleads with Ritchie.

"I will know it when I see it," Ritchie says as he presses on to his destination.

Ritchie and Hunter 311 arrive at the cave murals.

Ritchie studies the murals, after a few minutes he points up to one of them. "Don't you notice something?"

The mural glistens slightly. The white writing stands out against a painted black background.

Ritchie throws his backpack on the ground and begins pulling tools out. "It's another farce. Look closely."

Hunter 311 tries to see what Ritchie is referring to. "I don't see what you are talking about."

Ritchie walks past him, Hunter 311 notices the paint scraper in his hand.

Hunter 311 is astounded. "What are you doing?" he tries to stop Ritchie by grabbing his hand holding the scraper.

Ritchie pulls away. "Just look!" He starts scraping the paint off the mural.

Hunter 311's eyes grow wide.

Ritchie continues to scrape.

The mural begins to show a picture beneath the law. A light blue color.

Hunter 311 spots another paint scraper in the bag, picks it up, and begins to scrape paint from the mural also.

The two scrape and scrape until the true mural beneath appears. When completely scraped the two step back and awe at their discovery.

The mural depicts a prophecy.

The prophecy shows floods forcing a mass of white peoples from the West onto the Colored Empire.

The two men conceive the meaning of the mural.

"Your people found out that whites would eventually come." Ritchie ponders the evidence. "Somewhere along the line down here this prophecy created a fear that turned into-

"Us," Hunter 311 finishes his statement, "Me."

"Look, we don't have time for therapy and coming to terms right now," Ritchie pokes fun at him.

"What?" Hunter 311 asks confused.

Ritchie begins to look at the murals together. "Just tell me what you see when you look at the murals now."

Hunter 311 looks closely at all three. "The first three are historical," he says. Then, points to the flood mural. "This one prophetic."

Ritchie puts the final piece of the puzzle together in his head. "And the mural in the secret cave is the possible outcome," he exclaims.

Hunter 311 nods in agreement, thinking about the implications, the meaning of the Empire, the Hunt, and his life.

Suddenly, a voice from inside the cave jolts them from their deep thoughts. "It is an outcome that will never happen!" Teecher's voice booms.

VII

The Prophecy

1

Hunter 311 and Ritchie swing around to see Teecher standing just inside the cave, pointing a giant 21st century assault rifle at them. He is bloody, charred, and pissed.

Hunter 311 glances at a disguised Ritchie.

"I told you that you were soft," Teecher hisses before spitting on the ground. He walks forward, shaking his head and pointing his gun back and forth at both of them.

Hunter 311 begins to act, "Teecher! You are alive!"

The old Teecher stops and stares at him coldly.

Hunter 311 continues. "This fellow Hunter and I were just examining this..." He looks at the new mural, "vandalism of our sacred—"

"Shut up fool!" Teecher snaps. "You insult me by thinking I could not tell my own race with at least one of my senses?"

Hunter 311's reaction is a mix of fear and amazement.

Ritchie stays silent.

"How can you tell?" Hunter 311 asks, glancing at Ritchie.

Teecher sneers at his student. "Any real Hunter could have told merely by their smell! They require no hair oil. Do his dreads smell of it?"

Hunter 311 can't help but take a whiff toward Ritchie.

"Some Hunter," Teecher comments. He looks at the scraped mural. "As for this vandalism you are examining, it sure looks a lot like conspiring with a white to destroy the law on the Bible Wall!"

Hunter 311 decides to enlighten Teecher. "Look sir. The law was painted over the original mural!" Hunter 311 points up at it. "There has been some—"

"I said shut up!" Teecher takes a moment before going on. "Get away from it," he orders.

The two walk slowly toward the other side of the cave area.

175

Teecher approaches the scraped mural. "It is amazing how intelligent this white is and what he is capable of. Making it look like a mural is beneath under our law." Teecher rubs his finger on the surface of the new image. "The Senators and King will not be able to ignore this! It is obvious you are a white spy sent from an invading force to undermine our ways and beliefs, creating defeat within us for sure."

Ritchie snickers. "Too bad I'm the last of my kind."

"I actually hope so very much," Teecher says before turning back around, "So this will be all over once I kill you."

Ritchie glares at Teecher.

"But finding you in your disguise will get the army Vote regardless." Teecher cocks the large weapon. "Get over here Hunter," Teecher orders Hunter 311 to his side.

Hunter 311 knows his old teacher, he complies quickly, leaving Ritchie alone in harm's way.

Teecher smiles at the pitiful rookie Hunter before his attention once again turns to Ritchie. "And if you are the only one, then I can go back to worrying about hunting monkeys again." Teecher aims his rifle at Ritchie.

In an instant, Ritchie pulls a machine pistol from his Hunter coat and fires at Teecher.

Teecher dodges the bullets by rolling away from the gunfire, but instantly fires back.

Ritchie scrambles away into the dimness of the cavern and hides behind an area of protruding rock in the cave wall. "Run!" he yells to Hunter 311.

Hunter 311 soars into a dark nook of the cave while Ritchie and Teecher proceed with their fire fight. Both begin to shoot toward each other repeatedly. After only a few seconds both men need to reload.

"You alright?" Ritchie shouts to Hunter 311.

"Yes," Hunter 311 responds. "Just get out of here!"

Ritchie sees the entrance, but hesitates. "What about you?" he shouts back.

"Forget about me! You are the last of your kind! Now go!"

Ritchie thinks about it.

"I said go!" Hunter 311 screams.

"We'll see each other again buddy!" Ritchie yells before running full speed to the cave exit. Once through the doorway, he fires at Teecher from outside the bunker door.

Teecher returns fire, but Ritchie slips back and the bullets hit the door jam.

"Stay back!" Ritchie screams before rolling a grenade right at Teecher.

The old Hunter sees the weapon coming and dives out of the way, the grenade hits the wall and explodes. The explosion sends shock waves throughout the underground cavern and the cave fills with dust and smoke.

2

The fleet of White Hunters returns to the city, passing the short Empire walls. The Brigade Captain leads them, radio in hand. "Yes, sir," he speaks. "All areas checked. No sign of them. Seven savages were found and eliminated." Brigade Captain hears a faint sound of an engine. "What is—" is all he has time to say.

Suddenly, the city gate explodes open. Ritchie plows through the remains of the gate on a 2012 Buell motorcycle. He already has his machine pistol aimed.

Brigade Captain is stunned, frozen. Some of the White Hunters react by drawing their projectile weapons firing.

Ritchie veers right to avoid the bullets while returning fire, his bullets slam into three White Hunter's foreheads. Ritchie then holsters his pistol and begins throwing grenades at the fleet. Two explosions rock the fleet! Three White Hunters are blown apart. The remaining White Hunters seek cover.

Ritchie gives them the middle finger and barrels away on the motorcycle.

The Hunters are in disarray, some attempt to collect themselves.

Brigade Captain pulls up, half out of his car and screaming orders to the other Hunters. "Go! Go! Get him!"

While still full throttled, Ritchie looks back only for a second.

Brigade Captain burns out in pursuit and the remaining Hunters follow.

3

King Amses sits in his recliner in his throne room. Several women massage him, another feeds him fruit.

Harold sits off reading a book.

Suddenly, the room is shook by explosions. The King catches himself, eyes wide. "What is that?"

The throne room doors open and the King's guards escort Lieutenant Hunter in.

"My King!" Lieutenant Hunter declares, "The white is here! He is fighting the Hunter fleet!"

King Amses looks as if he realizes the mistake he has made. "Oh my," he utters.

4

"A race!" The young 5-year old Pupil 318 yells as he jumps up and down. "A race with loud lights!"

The other Pupils in the dorm emerge from their rooms.

"What is he saying?" Pupil 316 appears holding his blanket and rubbing his eyes.

Suddenly, Pupil 315 slams through the sliding doors. "Did you hear that?" he screams.

The children look at him wide eyed.

"Yes," Hunter 317 asks, "What is it?"

"It was a race!" Pupil 318 exclaims.

"Where?" Pupil 315 orders the young boy to tell him.

Pupil 318 skips over to the window, where he had been looking out a small crack in the sill, and pushes the button to trigger the window to slide open.

"Look!" Pupil 317 points out into the city.

In the distance they see the Hunter fleet chasing Ritchie, explosions all around, and gun fire bursting.

"A white man," Pupil 315 says in disbelief.

5

Teecher and Hunter 311 both lay unconscious on the sacred Temple cave floor. Explosions and gunshots ring out in the distance.

6

Tysheka vacuums her bedroom floor. The music is so loud that she does not hear the explosions and gunshots that have begun to ring out nearby.

"Yes," she exclaims as she begins to dance while cleaning.

7

Cicily awakens inside Crystal's tiny apartment, her head pounding.

"What was that?" Monique asks aloud.

"I don't know," Crystal answers. "I've never heard anything like that before."

Both women instinctually look to Cicily.

"Well don't look at me," Cicily announces as she realizes her friend's eyes are on her. She too looks around the room and to the window. "I don't know everything, you know. All I know is something loud woke me up." She rubs her aching head.

Crystal gets up and quickly locks her door. "Let's just stay here in my apartment just in case."

"Wow," Monique points to the door, "You can make it so the door won't open?"

"New model," Crystal says, "Didn't have the slightest idea what I'd ever use it for until now."

8

"I don't see them anymore," Pupil 318 says as he stares out of the window.

"They're gone," Pupil 315 snaps. "And like some measly citizen, there is nothing we can do about it." He punches the wall.

"Calm down," Pupil 316 says.

"What did I tell you about worrying about me?" Pupil 315 spins around and eyes Pupil 316.

Both twins back away from the older Pupil.

"I am going to work out next door," Pupil 315 says before storming out of the dorm.

The Pupils turn to the window and watches the city gate burn.

9

Ritchie pushes his Buell through a grassy plain West of the city of the Colored Empire. At least twenty Hunter vehicles pursue him. He aims behind without looking, pulling three shots off at a time. Three Hunter vehicles are struck, the bullets hit the drivers in the head through the windshields. Two of the Hunter vehicles flip, the other barrels aimlessly to a stop in a patch of grass.

Ritchie holsters his pistol and pushes on.

The Hunter fleet, now at least one quarter gone, continues to follow their target.

Ritchie veers left abruptly, then turns, ripping on the clutch. All of a sudden his motorcycle springs up high in the air. Brigade Captain sees the motorcycle's flight. He and his pit bull look at each other. Ritchie lands perfectly not stopping.

The Hunter fleet pursues.

Suddenly, Ritchie skids to a stop, turns around and watches.

The Hunter fleet pushes harder. The first cars reach the spot where Ritchie ramped, and Brigade Captain watches them soar up into the air and then down over the hillcrest. "Get ready for a jump!" he yells into his radio. Just then he and the second set of Hunter vehicles hit the jump and blow the grass off a man-made ramp.

"Oh no," Brigade Captain whispers as he has seen the ramp too late. His car jolts up into the air and down into a giant hole which Ritchie had covered in grass. The Captain's vehicle drops down thirty feet onto several cars already smashed at the bottom. The Hunter's do not have time to get out of their cars before the second set of vehicles smash them.

Brigade Captain's vehicle bounces off two other cars and slams into the wall of the giant hole. Several more Hunter vehicles rain down onto the massive car pileup.

Ritchie puts his motorcycle on the kickstand and struts to the trap he set.

Inside the giant hole, the Hunters that are capable have begun to get out of their cars. Some are already trying to find a way out the huge hole. A couple use their spears to pull themselves out, but see the dirt is too wet to be of any use. A few Hunters' pit bulls join them as they try in vain to scamper up the steep side of the wall.

Ritchie peers down. "That should be all of them," he says to himself.

The Hunters spot him. Several attempt projectile attacks.

Ritchie simply steps back and the projectiles fly over his head and land behind him.

Brigade Captain gets out of his car, bleeding from the head. His dog lay still in the car behind him. The Captain touches the ground and smells his finger. "We have to get out!" he starts yelling. "Don't you smell that?" He frantically tries to dig up the wall with his hands, but slides down like the rest. He activates his claw-arm and tries to climb up, still in vain.

Above the hole Ritchie turns away and smiles. He reveals a match, examining the antique, the light thin splintered wood, the round head smelling of sulfur, a product of a civilization long gone. He ponders about that world, those people, and how they let their world turn to this. He lights the match at last on his teeth, peering at the flame for only a moment before tossing it behind him.

Huge flames shoot from the hole. The sounds of men's screams are drowned out by Ritchie starting his motorcycle. He does not look back before speeding away.

10

Hunter 311 awakens alone in the temple. He turns to the cave exit, but the grenade blast has caused a huge pile of rocks and boulders to crash down and fill the doorway.

"Skeet!" Hunter 311 cusses. He rises and begins to look around. "There has to be another way out of here," he says to himself.

A glisten of metal catches his eye and he spots an old rusted grate. "The old air system!" he exclaims as he rushes over to it and rips it from the cave wall. Inside is a dark compact duct running outward into the darkness of the unknown. He pushes a button on his belt and two flashlights power up on his shoulders.

Hunter 311 turns back one last time before crawling into the duct and disappearing. Once inside his lights brightly illuminate the shaft ahead of him. He sees that the duct begins to ascend ahead of him.

"Surface, here I come," he says as he begins to crawl.

11

"So you know you were supposed to advise me correctly then?" the King screams at Harold.

Harold's eyes are wide with fear. He mumbles and stutters out an answer. "Yes, my King," he takes a huge gulp of air, "But, I never thought he would come into the city like this. In such a swift fashion as well."

The King turns to the Senators and Head White Hunters. "How many times am I going to have to come to Politic Hill today?"

The two groups stand silent.

The King grabs the gun from the closest hunter to him, Lieutenant Hunter, and turns shooting Harold in the face. The advisor's body slumps to the floor.

Everyone is stunned, some Senators distraught.

"No need for bad advice right now," the King concludes.

Blood pours from the giant hole in Harold's face. Everyone looks down at him for a second, except the King. He seems to have forgotten his advisor already, handing the gun back to the Lieutenant who takes it back and replaces it in his holster.

The King then turns to the two groups and speaks. "I don't know what is going on here, but between you two groups of highly experienced men, you better solve it."

The Senators and Head White Hunters look at each other.

"Do I make myself clear?" the King hisses.

All nod, or verbal answer in agreement.

"Good, now I am going back to my throne." The King steps over his advisor's body. "And get someone to clean him up."

12

Hunter 311 finally reaches the end of the rising tunnel of air duct, and sees another air grate ahead of him. He quickly crawls to the grate and punches it open. He doesn't even look around before falling out of the duct onto cold concrete.

"Where in Godallah am I?" he asks himself as he rises and looks around.

He is in a long giant underground room. The ceiling must be at least thirty feet high, with several intricate domes and trim on it. Huge pictures line the walls on one side, with stairs leading up at the end of the long room. On the opposite side of the pictures the room seems to drop off.

"What is this place?" Hunter 311 asks aloud again as he peers into the room's drop off. Two long metal beams with wood planks running in between them run perfectly straight through the drop off. He notices the drop off and metal beams keep going on both sides of the long room, going further into large tunnels that curve off and disappear into the darkness.

Hunter 311 ponders on which way to go. "I need to go up," he says. He jogs toward the stairs, but a picture on the wall catches his eye.

He stops and reads aloud, "Black Eyed Peas, Live at Atlantic Hall, Friday, October 29, 2014." The picture is of three colored men and a white woman. They are holding her up, but seemingly embracing her in an intimate manner.

Hunter 311's eyes stay frozen on the picture. He studies the white woman's features, her fair skin, blue eyes, blonde hair. The colored men smile as they hold her.

"The way the world used to be," Hunter 311 whispers. He finally breaks himself free from the picture's hold on him and climbs the stairs.

After a short walk down a dusty gray hallway Hunter 311 comes to a turnstile and tries to scan his wrist as he would at

Empire transit systems. But the scanner is long dead, if it was ever a scanner at all. Instead, he merely jumps over the metal obstruction. On the other side is another room, much smaller than the first, but no exits anywhere. Hunter 311 looks around, only the word "SUBWAY" can barely be seen on the one of the walls.

There is a door in the corner and he tries to open it, but it has long been locked. Two swift kicks jar the old door open and a dank musty smell hits Hunter 311 in the face. The room is an old janitor closet: mop bucket, cleaning chemicals, tools, all rusted, molded, caked with dust and decay. But there is a metal ladder on the wall that leads up several feet to a pressurized hatch.

"Found ya," Hunter 311 exclaims. He climbs the ladder and easily opens the hatch into a tunnel rising at least 100 feet above him. He climbs up further, his lights again illuminating the tunnel above him as he goes. At the top of the ladder he sees the bottom of a manhole cover, the Empire emblem stamped on it.

"Finally," Hunter 311 grunts as he pushes up and moves the sewer cover.

The young Hunter emerges from a sewer hole on a side street. He puts the cover back on the hole and begins to walk away when shots ring out, bullets just miss him and ricochet off the cement. He spots a White Hunter perched on top of a building across the street with a sniper rifle.

"What the?" he asks aloud as the sniper takes more shots at him. This time he jumps out of the way and dashes into a side alley. He rests for a second. "Now why are Hunters trying to kill me?" he asks himself as he tries to catch his breath. "They must be helping Teecher!" After looking around he gets low and he continues down the alley.

13

Ritchie pulls over beside a creek. He stoops to drink some water and sees the reflection of a white man. Surprised, Ritchie rises and turns to the owner.

A huge muscular white man unlike anything he has ever seen before stands before him. He has extravagant clothes, furs and leathers, boots, and armor. A forged battle ax rests on his back, a sword on his side, machine gun strapped on his shoulder, and a semi-automatic Beretta on his belt. An obvious soldier.

The giant white warrior smiles at Ritchie. "Howdy," he says.

Ritchie is instantly scared. He has never seen a white with weapons since he came up to the surface. And never a young adult, nor someone dressed so intricately. Yet, one thing was for sure, Ritchie had heard some of the whites speaking some dialect of English, so he knew they could speak and communicate in their own way.

"Hello, I uh–" Ritchie says talking slowly so the warrior may understand him, points to himself. "I-am-Ritchie."

The white warrior laughs, then mocks Ritchie. "I-am-Bobby-Joe. Sergeant-Bobbie-Joe-Phillips."

Ritchie cannot believe it. "You speak English?"

"Well, of course," Bobby-Joe answers. "Isn't it the language of the good ole US of A?"

Ritchie smiles, then breaks out laughing with joy. "Well of course it is!" Ritchie hugs the giant warrior.

"OK, man," Bobby-Joe protests. "Not that friendly." Bobby-Joe gives Ritchie a polite but firm shove back.

"Sorry, sorry," Ritchie apologizes. "I have not seen a person like me, that can speak and think at all, in well, longer than I want to tell."

Bobby-Joe eyes Ritchie with a don't B.S. me look. "What are you talking about?"

Ritchie almost can't stand it. "Where are you from?"

Bobby-Joe pipes up. "I am Bobby-Joe, soldier in the Nebraskan Army of the old US of A."

Ritchie's eyes are wide. "Nebraskan Army?"

"Yes sir." Bobby-Joe replies with pride. "I'm on a scouting mission for the 7-States' encampment West of here." Bobby-Joe points behind him.

"Encampment?" Ritchie repeats.

"The survivors of the floods." Bobby-Joe explains. "It has been raining back home for months. Floods have wiped the plain states from Oklahoma on up right off the map. Forced the states to unite into a nation, and then forced what was left of the nation East."

Ritchie cannot believe it. "What seven states?"

Bobby-Joe smiles. "In the last 10 years we've united Nebraska, Oklahoma, Colorado, the Dakotas, Kansas, and Wyoming. Since then we have been on a mission to reunite all the states sir."

Ritchie looks behind the warrior. "People are alive out there?"

Bobby-Joe glances behind him as well. "In the plains? No. Everyone is here, at least the people that came with us when the floods hit. The others-" He thinks for a second, grimaces. "I am not sure if any could of survived."

"What about the other states West of the plains?" Ritchie inquires.

"After the war," Bobby-Joe answers, "when groups started uniting again, we took in any people from other states we encountered. My mother was actually from past the Montana border. It's just the mountain and Western states were completely annihilated in the war sir."

Ritchie is ecstatic. "This is the best thing I could have ever hoped for."

Bobby-Joe scowls at Ritchie.

"The fact that you are reuniting the states, of course," Ritchie adds.

Bobby-Joe nods in understanding. "We are not just uniting the states, but there are scholars among us collecting historical artifacts like books. Much of our history was lost in the World War III."

"You call it World War III?" Ritchie asks.

"That's what it was," Bobby-Joe replies.

"I can definitely help in that area. I can show you, give the cause, a very unimaginable amount of valuable assets that can help rebuild our country better and faster than you ever dreamed."

Bobby-Joe's eyebrows raise. "Really? Sounds good. But, how?"

"Follow me and I will show you." Ritchie begins to stalk West. "You will be getting an accommodation and promotion for scouting this out I am sure."

Bobby-Joe looks around for a second, shrugs, and then follows Ritchie over a small hill.

14

Tysheka finishes cleaning and turns off her music player. She goes to the kitchen area, opens a barren refrigerator, and takes out the only pristine item: the bottle of orange juice. She brings the bottle to the cabinet, retrieving a glass, and pours a couple of drinks in.

Tysheka is about to take a drink when she hears something in the back room. She leaves the glass. "Mom?"

She finds nothing, shakes her head, and turns back toward the kitchen. When she returns Teecher stands there holding her glass of juice.

"Hello my dear," he hisses. "I have heard so much about you."

15

Hunter 311 slips across an alley wall towards a street opening, waits for a second before sticking his head slowly around the corner. Citizens walk the streets, some in a daze, while others are panicking from the explosions and gunfire.

No sign of White Hunters. Yet, the vast street is too wide to traverse across easily, especially if sharpshooting hunters are perched on a rooftop nearby.

Hunter 311 steals back into the alley, thinking to himself. "How can I get around?" He has only one goal at this point: To make sure his sister, and especially his niece are safe. If Teecher knew anything about him, it was his love and thus weakness regarding his family.

Hunter 311 peeks out at the street again. Two Hunters have just rounded the street corner and are searching the street and alleyways. He looks back at where he came from for a moment, yet the young Hunter can hear the two patrolling White Hunters getting closer.

"Check that alley!" one orders the other.

Hunter 311 looks back, then up, and spots an old prewar fire escape on the side of the building he is leaning on.

"Good one," he compliments himself as he springs to the last rung on the fire escape ladder and pulls himself up.

One of the Hunters enters the alleyway just as Hunter 311 climbs the stairs of the fire escape silently.

"All clear," the Hunter states into his radio.

Hunter 311 reaches the rooftop, but stays low as he goes due to possible Hunters stationed in other high positions.

The first few roofs are very open, with little to no places for cover, making Hunter 311 very paranoid and alert. Yet, the next rooftop seems to start a series of cluttered rooftops, full of shanty buildings, tents, and other objects that could provide perfect cover.

"Welcome to Cretaceous Park!" a screechy old voice rings out behind him.

Hunter 311 jumps forward and swings around, ready for battle, or possibly to run. The voice belongs to an aged black sheep, dressed in dirty clothes of all different sizes and colors, with a top hat and cane. His white hair is shoved messily up into his old hat. His bushy white eyebrows raise up as he sees Hunter 311's badge.

"A Hunter, eh?" The man is not afraid. "Well, ain't no whites up here in Cretaceous Park." He chuckles like an old bird. "But I tell ya, we'd probably accept 'em here if they did come."

The old derelict motions for Hunter 311 to follow.

The young Hunter looks around in hesitation at first, then back, and toward the street, thinking about trying to travel on ground, before finally following the old man.

"Why do you call it Cretaceous Park?" Hunter 311 asks as he approaches the slow moving old man.

The black sheep turns. "Well, because it is full of dinosaurs the world has forgotten." The old man presents his town to Hunter 311 with a slow swoop of his hand.

For as far as the eye can see, hundreds, perhaps thousands of makeshift shacks, buildings, tents, line the rooftops. Countless people seem to go about their day, cooking food outside, talking amongst themselves, walking from one place to another.

"Yes, Cretaceous Park has become its own city," the old man informs Hunter 311. "Why, we have our own markets," he points to an area where a small farmer's market has been set up, yet most of the tables are barren of food. "We have a park," he points to a small area where grass has grown through the roof. A small group of children kicks a ball around the patch of grass.

"The grass growing through is a sign of instability," Hunter 311 tells the old man.

The black sheep laughs heartily. "Well beggars can't be choosers, young Hunter."

The two continue on. Hunter plans on walking right through Cretaceous Park, and by his calculations it seems it may get him fairly close to Cicely's.

"Why, we even have a public restroom," the old man points to an old port o potty. "We just have to get the men together to empty it weekly.

The smell hits Hunter 311 and he gasps, almost throwing up.

"It takes some getting used to," the old black sheep motions for him to follow.

Hunter 311 and the old man reach a gap between buildings. Several boards of different thickness and wood make a bridge to cross.

"Another safety hazard?" Hunter 311 asks.

The old derelict just laughs again before slowly crossing the bridge. The two men step down onto the next rooftop. This one is much like the first, yet primarily living quarters.

"So why is a White Hunter up here anyway," the black sheep asks Hunter 311 as he traverses the maze of makeshift buildings.

Hunter 311 does not know what to say.

"You're either hunting," the old man eyes him, "Or running."

Hunter 311 scoffs. "Why would I be running?" He does his best to be convincing.

"Who knows these days?" The old man waves to someone he knows. "Has it to do with the explosions and what not we heard earlier?"

Hunter 311 lights up. Ritchie! "Well, actually it does."

"Yea," the old man reaches the next building. "So what is going on? Our little hole in the wall Empire finally going down?" The black sheep chuckles at the thought as they cross the bridge of boards.

Hunter 311 does not know what to say again.

The old man steps onto the next rooftop, then turns to Hunter 311. "Whites caused the explosions?"

Hunter 311 again struggles with what to inform him. Finally, "Yes. One white, a very smart white, caused the explosions."

The black sheep seems to think about it for a few moments before walking on again.

"There's more," Hunter 311 follows behind him.

"Yeah." The old man answers, almost as if he doesn't want to hear.

"Yes," Hunter 311 casually blurts it out, "Our Empire is built on lies."

The black sheep stops and turns to him. "Really?"

"Yes, sometime during our time underground, or perhaps during the transition to the top our government altered the Bible, the sacred cave, to make it seem like whites were evil."

The old man just stares, listening, waiting.

"But the prophecy says we should be united with them," Hunter 311 trails off, not understanding the man's reaction to what he is saying.

"Is that right?" The black sheep comments before walking again.

Hunter 311 cannot understand why the man is not at least slightly bewildered. "Perhaps he is mad?" Hunter 311 thinks to himself. "Or he thinks I am mad."

"Wait," Hunter 311 calls out to him.

The black sheep stops, turns. "Yes?"

"Well, why are you not surprised at what I am saying? You see my badge, I am a White Hunter, do you not believe me?"

"Of course son." The old man just stands there again, watching, waiting.

"Well, what do you think?" Hunter 311 demands.

The black sheep smiles, takes off his top hat, his willowy white hair set free. "Fact is son. After a lifetime of the Empire lying to us, forsaking us, I don't think there is a person here that would surprise."

Hunter 311 looks out at Cretaceous Park. The people do not seem to be in the same state as the citizens on ground level. No cries of fear nor signs of shock. Individuals seem to be going about their regular day.

The black sheep puts his hat back on and turns away from Hunter 311. "My home is not far this way." He points to a branch of Cretaceous Park heading North. "Which way are you headed?"

"West," the young Hunter points towards Cecily's house.

The old man shakes his head in confirmation. "Goes on for quite some time that way, it does."

Hunter nods. "Nice talking to you, meeting you."

"Aye." The old man turns toward home.

Hunter begins onward.

"Young man," the black sheep's voice calls out.

Hunter turns back. "Yes?"

"It is all going to Hell, isn't it?" The wind whips through the rooftop, making his white hair fly up around behind him.

Hunter 311 just stares at the old black sheep, thinking about a summation of it all. Finally, he answers, "I believe it may be inevitable."

16

"What are you doing in my house?" Tysheka yells at Teecher.

He gives a casual smirk. "Just looking for my student. He gave me the slip somehow back at the Temple. You should know he is facing some very serious charges, high treason. He will shame your family."

"What have you done to him?" she screams.

"Not enough. Not yet." Teecher sneers.

"What do you want?" Tysheka asks as she begins to back away.

Teecher turns and grabs something from the living room table. "I know he frequents here often to see you two."

Tysheka sees he is holding a picture of her mother and her. She looks around. "Mom?" she calls out.

Teecher shakes his head. "No, not here I'm afraid. Just you and I."

Suddenly, Tysheka darts to the front door, grabbing the handle right as Teecher tackles her to the floor.

17

Hunter 311 reaches the last building that makes up the West side of the shanty town called Cretaceous Park. He edges between the final shack and its neighboring tent to see Cicily's block.

"Cretaceous Park was right here above my sister's place and I never knew it," Hunter 311 says to himself in wonder.

"No one down there notices us," a voice whispers off somewhere.

A deformed woman lies in the corner of the rooftop, newspapers wrapped about her mangled body.

Hunter 311 turns away and begins down the fire escape ladder.

18

"Family!" Teecher yells as he grabs Tysheka by the waist and slams her onto the couch. "It can often be such a liability."

Tysheka whips around and cowers back from him. "What do you want?"

Teecher towers over her. "Your uncle, where is he?"

"I don't know," Tysheka cries, "I have not seen him since we went out to eat yesterday."

Teecher snatches Tysheka's up by her hair. "We're going for a ride. The stake of the Empire may lie-" The buzzing sound from the front door interrupts his words.

Teecher throws Tysheka back onto the couch again. "Stay here. Maybe Mom has just joined the party."

The front door is still wide open. Nothing stirring near it, the wind whips into the apartment. Teecher stalks over to it slowly, one of his many knives already unsheathed and in stabbing position.

Tysheka watches in silence.

Teecher bends his neck as he approaches, but sees nothing outside. He looks back at her. "Don't move," he orders before heading out the door.

"Tysheka," Hunter 311 whispers from the back of the apartment.

Tysheka squints and spots her uncle crouching in the darkness of the hall.

"Come on honey," Hunter 311 whispers. "Hurry."

Tysheka darts from the couch. The front door still open, no sign of Teecher. She reaches her uncle.

"What is going on uncle?" Tysheka asks him.

"No time to explain." Hunter 311 escorts her to her mother's room. "I activated the front door. I can't believe it worked." The two go to the back window, already opened. He motions for her to go out and helps her through.

Teecher has checked the perimeter and is coming back through the front door.

"Where the?" He begins to scan the area. "Tysheka? Where are you?"

Hunter 311 scampers through the window and quickly leads his niece down the narrow alleyway.

"Quickly," he whispers as they turn onto an adjacent alley.

He spots a fire escape and takes his niece's hand. "Come on, we are safer on the rooftops."

"But," Tysheka hesitates. "You do know what is up there, don't you?"

"You know about Cretaceous Park?"

Tysheka nods. "Have a friend or two that ended up living up there." She snickers. "You've seen the cupboard in our house. We are constantly about to move up there ourselves."

Hunter 311 is offended. "No you would not, not ever."

Tysheka smiles at her uncle warmly.

Hunter 311 hears something behind them. "Hurry," he whispers as he helps her up to the fire escape ladder.

The two climb up to the rooftop to the edge of Cretaceous Park.

Hunter 311 helps her down onto the building's rooftop. "Is there a place you can go that is safe?" He asks.

"Yes," she takes his hand. "But I don't want to leave you."

Hunter 311 smiles at his niece. "I know." But shows his seriousness. "But that man wants to kill me. And he obviously will hurt you and your mother in order to get to me, so the safest possible situation is for you to go to an unknown safe place away from me."

Tysheka almost stomps her foot, but gives in. "I met a boy a few weeks ago, well I've known him from school for a couple years now. Anyway, no one knows I even know him. Not mom or anyone."

"Perfect. Where does he live?"

"A few blocks down from here," she points the direction.

"Let's go," Hunter 311 leads his niece through Cretaceous Park.

"But, where are you going?"

Hunter 311 looks back seriously. "Back to the Academy. I know at least one person there who may be able to help me."

19

Teecher stalks down an alley way. He reaches into his utility belt and grabs his radio. After punching in a secret code he pushes the talk button. "Radioing in. Teecher here. Radioing in."

The radio fuzzes for a second before Sergeant Hunter's voice comes back. "Teecher? Is that you?"

"Yes, it's me."

"You're not dead!" the old Sergeant's voice says.

"Of course not," he replies matter if factly. "Listen. I am in the city. Playing cat and mouse with my latest graduate. I just encountered both of them. The white is on the run."

"Yes," the Sergeant chimes in. "The majority of the fleet are after him."

"That's good. If they don't kill him I will after I take care of 311." Teecher grips the radio tight.

"Several Hunters are in the city looking for 311 as well," the Sergeant voice crackles.

"Just tell them to stay out of my way," Teecher hisses. "He is my problem."

There is silence for a moment.

Sergeant's voice comes through again. "He has become a problem for the entire Empire. What is your plan? Why have you not terminated 311 already? Footage shows you have been in close proximity to him several times already."

"I plan on destroying the other temple forever," Teecher sneers into his radio. "As it should have been long ago!"

More silence.

Finally, "What should we tell the Senators?" Sergeant Hunter asks.

"Nothing! They are the weak and powerless men who have put us in this position! Just make sure they kill the white. He is the last of his kind!"

20

Sergeant Hunter switches his radio off and places it in a drawer. He looks up at the other Head White Hunters sitting in front of his desk.

"He should not be running around the city like some rogue!" Deputy Hunter exclaims.

The other Hunters nod their heads.

There is a knock at the Sergeant office door.

"Come in," the Sergeant commands.

The sully group of Senators scramble inside the room. Each places himself in an unoccupied chair or nook of the room in preparation for a discussion.

Senator Makin stands in the center of the room and begins. "What are we to do?" He asks, addressing the two groups.

"A group of Hunters are tracking Hunter 311, the rest are pursuing the white now. What else is there to do?" Senator Mathis replies.

"Something doesn't seem right," Lieutenant Hunter grimaces. "Perhaps we should have not sent so many after the white?"

Senator Harlow Williams steps in the conversation. "You are all doubting yourselves right now. That is one of the goals of terrorism. To create fear, to create doubt in the ability to protect oneself."

Deputy Hunter laughs. "You are on a terrorism kick now? What, did you look it up since the King thinks the white is some black terrorist in disguise?"

Senator Mathis holds up his hand. "Look, the white was in all likelihood, escaping from the city. Now that the Hunters chased him off, it is very unlikely he will return tonight. Let us leave Politic Hill for the night and meet first thing in the morning to devise a plan of defense and action."

"All agreed?" Deputy Hunter democratically asks the group.

"Aye," the men all answer.

21

"I don't need to go to any hospital!" Demetrious screams at his parents. "There is danger, real danger!"

His mother sits nearby in a chair, dressed in an elaborate white dress. She does not even look at him. "Calm down," his mother tells him in a dull tone.

His father paces back and forth, rubbing his single lock of thick hair atop his otherwise bald head. He wears a lab coat and shiny gold wire glasses.

"Haven't you ever heard explosions before?"

"Well, yes," his father stops pacing. "When I set up that mining lab years ago."

"And we all did on the recording played at yesterday's Debate." Demetrious pleas, "So what are we waiting for?"

His family simply stare at him.

Demetrious kicks the living room wall. "We need to get out of here! Out of the city I am telling you! No one in the government will give us answers. I can't even find a single White Hunter–" Demetrious notices Tysheka outside the window.

"I think we should wait and see what happens Demetrious," his father protests.

Demetrious waves him on. "Ya, ya, alright." And walks out of the living room.

His father cannot believe how quickly his son's tirade ended. "OK?"

Demetrious follows the windows of his home until he gets to the boy's bedroom and opens the window next to his bed. "Tysheka, what is going on?"

Tysheka quickly looks around. "Can I come in? It's an emergency."

"Yeah, of course," Demetrious says, then helps her in.

Once in she pleads, "Lock all your windows please!"

"OK," he begins to close and lock them. "What is wrong?"

"You're not going to believe me."

22

Hunter 311 sees his niece go through the window and lets out a breath of relief. He turns back toward Cretaceous Park. The mass of stress returns as he begins to think about what he should do next.

"Dropped off the niece somewhere safe did you?" Teecher leans against a shanty house several feet away.

Hunter 311 staggers back from him, shaking his head.

"You should know you can't hide from me," Teecher exclaims, "I am, after all, your Teecher." Teecher draws his Hunter crossbow and fires at Hunter 311 repeatedly. The arrows soar toward him, several striking buildings and going over the rooftop ledge, yet one hits a vagrant of Cretaceous Park, and two sink into Hunter 311's shoulder.

Hunter 311 slams back onto the rooftop ledge and slides over, leaving a large smear of blood on the bricks of the ledge wall.

Teecher runs to the ledge to find an empty fire escape, Hunter 311's blood trailing down to the street below. He barely catches a glimpse of him disappearing around an alley corner.

"The Hunt is on again!" Teecher exclaims before jumping down the fire escape.

23

"I'm ready to change my life," Cicily states aloud.

Her girlfriends all scoff over her comment.

"I've heard that before," Monique says.

"It's different this time." Cicily takes her BarCard from her purse and walks to a window. "I'm getting rid of this first."

"What?" Monique gasps. "You won't be able to get into any bar until next quarter when the government issues new BarCards!"

Cicily tosses it out the window, it falls and shatters to pieces on the street below. "And I won't be getting another one then either. I need to be there for my daughter. Finally."

"Because of what's happening?" Crystal asks.

"No, I've been thinking about it for a long time."

"You can still scan your hand account if you change your mind anyway," Monique quips.

Crystal and Cicily give each other a look, both thinking about Cicily's empty hand account.

"I think we should get out of the city," Crystal says finally.

Cicily smacks her lips. "And go where?"

"We could go to the annexed area down South," Monique retorts.

"That's actually a really good idea," Cicily mutters.

"What? Are you serious?" Crystal joins her at the window and they both look down onto the street below.

Several people seem to roam the street. Some look for loved ones, while others are delirious or injured. The city gate still burns in the distance and two other fires burn brightly in the distance of the Empire city.

"What is going on?" Cicily asks.

No one has an answer.

"I don't know," Crystal says finally.

24

Hunter 311 runs full speed through an alley backdoor into a long hallway of sleek offices. He hears the loud thumping of music and his eyes shoot to the swinging doors at the end of the hall.

"Club fun," he says as he dashes to the doors and slams through.

Teecher enters the alley door and casually walks down the hall and through the swinging doors.

The club is full of people, so much in fact that Hunter 311 has to squeeze through the masses, touching each drugged out, gyrating person.

Open rooms line the club, each space dedicated to the various pleasures of life. Several people lounge around the first room, smoke pouring from the giant hookah pipe built in the wall. The next room a fantasy of naked flesh, human secretion, and free love for all. Each room holds the next substance or activity, pleasure zones, pastimes deemed vital to Empire life.

Hunter 311 passes each staple of pleasure, lucky enough to not have any idea what each entails, and thus saving him from the addictive and remarkable attributes each holds.

Teecher spots Hunter 311 going for the front entrance and plows his way through the crowd toward him. He knocks people aside, some hitting others and falling down their tiny personal space to the floor below.

Hunter 311 reaches the entrance and darts onto the street. He quickly looks around. "Only a couple of blocks now." He runs across the street and into the alley, no time to look in all directions like he wants to.

Teecher barges out of the club entrance, spots his once time pupil instantly and barrels to the alleyway

Hunter 311 reaches the Hunter Academy courtyard, but stops to check the perimeter. He sees no sign of Hunters, and only a few citizens walking or loitering aimlessly. Hunter 311 glances back to see Teecher stalking towards him, staring menacingly with that bully mug.

"Neezylife!" A voice booms right behind Hunter 311. He swings around to face a huge commercial image on the wall of the building he was leaning on. A man dressed in a purple outfit, gold teeth, cane, and top hat points at Hunter 311. "Live the playa life! Live the pimp life! Live the Neezylife!" He shoves a NeezyCola at Hunter 311.

Hunter 311 kicks the wall, the image fizzles and then zaps out. He dashes across the courtyard and up the Hunter Academy steps.

Teecher approaches, fiddles with something on the wall, and the commercial beams up again.

"Neezylife!" The commercial plays again.

25

In a flash there was something in Monique's eyes. She was oddly frozen for a few moments, as if receiving a signal from afar perhaps, then all of a sudden she clicked back on. "You know I think you should avoid the bars more Cil."

Cicliy and Crystal both look up and around as if the voice came from some enigmatic fourth party somewhere in the room. Then they both look at Monique.

"What?" Monique says. "I think I should too."

"Whoa!" Crystal almost shouts. "Where is this coming from?"

Monique throws her hands up slightly. "I am just thinking you know?"

"It's just that I have known you since you were five years old and nothing, I mean nothing has ever come out of your mouth in the category as what you just said."

"Well, maybe I am suddenly thinking differently." Monique turns in her chair and thinks for a second. "Like I may want to settle down soon too."

"Marriage?" Crystal cannot believe it.

"I know it is hard to find a good man," Monique admits.

Cicily laughs. "Difficult doesn't quite describe it."

26

Gardner peers into a microscope in the agricultural lab of the Hunter Academy.

The automated warning voice booms over the loudspeakers. "All vital personnel to their stations! Code white! All Hunters are on active duty. Repeat all vital personnel to their stations!"

Gardner shakes his head. "What the white is going on 311?" He says to himself.

"A huge, elaborate system of lies best describes it," Hunter 311 answers from behind Gardner.

Gardner startles, then spins around. "Boy, what is happening?"

"I found about all the lies the Empire has spun for so long, and now they want me dead."

A loud alarm begins to wail.

"You were seen coming here?" Gardner asks in terror.

Hunter 311 tells him, "Teecher followed me; I couldn't lose him this time."

Suddenly gun shots ring out and ricochet off the lab tables. Gardner ducks, while Hunter 311 dives behind a metal cabinet.

Teecher steps into the lab, begins to reload the shotgun. "Come to get help from your old buddy, did you? Maybe some of those grow tips will help you dodge these shells."

In a flash Hunter 311 hits Teecher from the side, tackling him to the ground.

Teecher laughs and swings the shotgun around hitting Hunter 311 in the side of the head. He instantly goes to his knees, dizzy.

"Stop!" Gardner screams as he rushes Teecher and knees him in the gut.

Teecher takes the strike and smiles. "How long you been wanting to do that?" He jabs Gardner in his nose, blood pours instantly from his nostrils. Teecher grabs Gardner by his gray dreads. "I will take pleasure in killing you as well, old traitor!" Teecher draws his sword and raises it above his head.

Gardner stays still, crouching and holding his bleeding nose.

Hunter 311 jumps on Teecher's back, and starts to choke him.

"Run Gardner! Go!" Hunter 311 grits through his teeth as he tries to squeeze the choke harder.

"No," Gardner rises, "I will—"

Teecher pulls the trigger of his shotgun, the blast echoes loudly through the lab.

Hunter 311 begins to let go of his choke as he sees Gardner fall to his knees again. His eyes grow wide, then seem to fade before he falls to the side dead. Blood rushes from the giant hole in his chest.

"No!" Hunter 311 screams.

Teecher sees his chance, flips Hunter 311 over his shoulder, and aims at him. Hunter 311 rolls and Teecher tries shooting him, but the bullets miss and hit a pressurized tank. The dials on all the tanks start to shoot up into the red zones.

"Shit," Teecher says before dashing out the lab doors.

Hunter 311 sees the fire consuming the bulging tanks. He quickly looks around and spots the open lab freezer. In an instant he runs for it, dives inside and slams the door shut over him.

A huge explosion consumes the lab.

27

"Did you hear that?" Hunter 309 asks Hunter 302.

Hunter 302 wipes his middle-aged brow. "Probably just the fire getting to a fuel source or a pressurized tank."

Hunter 309 is much younger, and is not listening to his older counterpart. "I think it came from the Academy!"

"Nonsense," Hunter 302 turns the other way. "We should check this perimeter again."

Hunter 309 is already is a trot towards the Academy. "I will meet you when you come back around."

Hunter 302 shakes his head. "What has gotten into this young generation?"

28

"A louder sound!" Pupil 318 exclaims.

"That was close!" Pupil 317 says.

"More than close," Pupil 316 corrects, "It shook the building."

"That's because it was in the building," Pupil 315 begins to quickly gear up.

"What are you doing?" Pupil 316 demands.

"I am going to investigate," Pupil 315 says as he finishes putting on his armor and weapons.

"You are supposed to stay inside the Academy!" Pupil 316 reminds him.

"I just told you that came from somewhere inside the building!" The older Pupil begins for the door but stops. "None of you follow me or come out of the dorm. Do you understand?"

All of them look reluctant in saying yes, but Pupil 315 knows none of them have the guts to leave anyway. He disappears out of the dorm doors, the glass closing behind him.

29

The agricultural wing's automatic fire extinguisher system consumes the entire lab in thick white suffocation, killing the flames almost instantly.

Hunter 309 peers around the corner at the lab, the extinguishers still jet their white sprays. He spots the terminal, hits the red button to stop the extinguishers.

"What in DeShawn's name?" Hunter 309 observes carefully as he enters the recently charred room. The thick white extinguisher substance covers everything. But the charred remains of the lab's objects can be seen in places.

Suddenly, Hunter 309 hears a thud in the back of the lab. He spots a huge drop-in freezer and draws his Hunter's pistol. "Who's there?" His voice quivers.

He hears nothing and draws closer to the charred freezer. "I said is anyone there?" He inches closer and peers over the freezer to look behind it.

Up comes the freezer door, hitting him in his chin and knocking him back.

Hunter 311 pops out of the freezer, thankful to be alive, and looks around. He sees Hunter 309 laying in front of the freezer, out cold.

"309," Hunter 311 shakes his head. "I was lucky to run into you." He crouches down and takes his pistol. "When I saw you become Hunter I knew even I could."

Hunter 311 spots Gardner's charred body, then runs out of the lab.

30

Teecher lies in wait from across the courtyard of the Hunter Academy. He points his high-tech binoculars at the entrance of the building.

"Any time now you slippery bastard," Teecher zooms in on the doors. "Give you that, you are definitely slippery."

Hunter 311 emerges from the doors, looks around quickly before descending the steps.

"Yes, now show me where it is," Teecher hisses. "Lead me right to it!"

31

Pupil 315 peers around the corner of the lab hallway. He spots the burnt lab room and draws his student pistol.

"Remember your training," he whispers to himself before bursting around the corner.

The lab is empty, the white fire extinguisher substance still covers most everything.

"Outta my way!" Someone yells as they slam past the young Pupil.

Pupil 315 catches himself against the wall just in time to see Hunter 309 disappear around the corner and out of the lab.

Pupil 315 shakes his head and returns to investigating. He spots the open freezer with no white inside it. Then he sees Gardner's charred body. His eyes widen at the sight of it. He peers closer before walking up and kneeling over it.

"What are you doing?" A booming voice calls out over him. They young man almost falls over, but snaps to his feet.

The slender middle-aged Hunter 306 stands before him, with his pistol drawn.

"I-I heard the same loud boom as I did when the white smashed through the city gate," Pupil 315 turns back in the direction of the incident as he explains.

"I know. I know." Hunter 306 stammers. "I heard it too." He quickly looks around. "What did you see?"

"Um," Pupil 315 begins to stutter. "Nothing. Just the lab like this, oh and the freezer over there was open," he points to the freezer, then looks back down at Gardner's body. "And then him."

Hunter 306 looks back down as well. "It's Gardner. What in DeShawn's name happened here?"

Pupil 315 looks around again. "I don't know."

"OK, get back to your dorm," Hunter 306 orders.

"Yes, sir," Pupil 315 replies and leaves immediately.

Hunter 306 thinks for a second before pulling his radio out. "Come in Sergeant." The radio buzzes and then the Sarge's voice comes back. "Yes?"

"Now we have trouble here in the Academy. For the life of me I can't figure it out, but someone, the white I presume, destroyed one of agricultural labs. The fire extinguisher system put it out and completely contained it, but Hunter 281 is dead."

The radio is silent for a second. "It could have been 311 as well. Continue the search."

Hunter 306 responds. "Yes, sir."

32

Senator Mathis holds the front door of the Politic Hill building as the other Senators file out.

"I cannot believe he came into the city," Senator Makin complains.

"A day like this calls for a drink!" Senator Mathis adds.

Senator Mathis' radio rings. "What now?" He answers it, "Yes?"

The radio buzzes and Sergeant Hunter's voice comes through. "Senators. Are you leaving the Capitol Building?"

"Yes, why?" Mathis answers.

More static before, "There's been another explosion in the city."

"Another?" Senator Makin cries.

"But the white has fled the city!" Senator Mathis pleas.

"We don't know the cause, Hunter 306 handles security and runs the cameras, but he is out with the fleet," the Sergeant radios. "But there was an explosion in the agricultural wing of the Academy. Luckily the fire extinguisher system put the fire out."

"If only the rest of the city had such systems!" Senator Makin quips.

"At least the holy structure is saved," the Sergeant sends back.

All of a sudden Hunter 311 stands before them.

The Senators stumbled back from his figure almost appearing out of nowhere.

"I need to talk with you," he staggers toward them, out of breath. "I have to tell you. Something is going on."

"Calm down young Hunter," Senator Makin suggests.

Senator MAthis shuts his radio off and puts it in his pocket. "What is it?" He asks, then notices his wounds. "You are bleeding son."

"I used to think you Senators were against us," Hunter 311 rambles. "But now I think you are the only people I can trust."

"Tell us what has happened," Senator Mathis says kindly.

Hunter 311 looks behind him. "It is the sacred cave. Someone has painted over the murals, and blocked off a portion of the cave." He turns back to the Senators. "The entire basis of our civilization is a lie."

The Senators smile at him.

"Young Hunter," Senator Mathis says. "It is a necessary lie."

Hunter 311 begins to back away from them. "You," he stutters, "You know about everything already."

"Well of course we do," Senator Makin replies. "It was our idea to begin with."

Out of nowhere the Head White Hunters appear.

Senator Mathis explains, "We were all young men then, most involved are now dead and gone. But, the Head Hunters, the Senators, and one scientist we called the Engineer were the only individuals who knew the truth. Since then only a handful of vital government employees know as well."

"You must understand," Lieutenant Hunter declares. "It was done in order to prevent the destruction of civilization again."

"Whites have been the destructors of our world since Hammurabi, a white king who existed near the beginning of time," Senator Mathis adds.

"And their pattern of destruction cycled again and again," Sergeant Hunter states. He puts his arm on Hunter 311's shoulder. "It had to be done. You must understand."

Hunter 311 backs away faster now. "No!"

He yells at them as he runs toward another alley.

The Head White Hunters draw their weapons and attack the fleeing young Hunter. Several other Hunters appear and begin to chase him.

Hunter 311 reaches the alley, spots a fire escape ladder and climbs up. The Hunters chasing him run past the ladder and he watches them disappear around a corner. The young Hunter climbs all the way up to the building's roof.

From there he can see the entire city. He looks out, wondering where Tysheka and Cicily are. He spots the city gate blown apart by Ritchie's escape.

Just then Hunter 311 hears a click, and feels a cold barrel on his cheek. He looks over to find Teecher with a gun on his face.

"Thought you could get away from your fate?"

Hunter 311 does not answer.

"Move," Teecher orders him.

33

"Where are you taking me?" Bobby-Joe asks Ritchie.

"To my home," Ritchie replies as they descend into a small valley filled with large white boulders. Ritchie approaches one and touches it, activating a hidden door that slowly rises from the ground.

Bobby-Joe crouches staring at the door in wonder. "How did you do that?"

"Technology," Ritchie says before entering the door. "A collection of the most prolific technologies of our past, as well as some created down here over the years."

The giant warrior stands frozen still not sure about the door.

"Come on in Bobby-Joe." Ritchie beckons him.

Again, Bobby-Joe scopes left, then right and behind before entering the doorway. Once in the door lowers back into the ground, the two men disappear.

Inside, Ritchie and Bobby-Joe descend in an elevator. Bobby-Joe crouches low in the corner, not liking the fact he is descending into the ground in a metal box. "What is this?" He asks in terror.

Ritchie approaches Bobby-Joe and assures him, "Everything is fine. It just goes up and down. A way into a safe bunker, like the one your ancestors stayed in to be safe from the nuclear fallout."

Bobby-Joe gives him a "that doesn't help look."

Upon touching down, the door opens, and Bobby-Joe almost crawls from the elevator.

Once outside, he looks back. "Any other way back up?"

"I am afraid not," Ritchie says.

Bobby-Joe shakes his head. Then he begins to look around. He has seen his share of the Nebraskan Military Technology, but he has never seen anything like this.

Ritchie's bunker is a wonderland of technology and objects he can only guess what they are for. Screens line all the walls. Mechanical gadgets fill the room, some even the size of large appliances.

"What is this place?" Bobby-Joe asks.

Ritchie looks around too. "My ancestors were inventors. So you could call this the Mecca of, well, inventions."

Bobby-Joe scopes the marvels.

On the table just in front of him are several objects that seem to interest him. He decides to grab a wheel with a string connected to it.

"It's called a yo-yo," Ritchie tells him. "It's a fun activity. Let me show you."

Bobby-Joe hands him the yo-yo.

Ritchie slips his finger through the loop and begins spinning it down and up.

Bobby-Joe scratches his head. "So what's the point?"

"It's just fun to go up and down I guess. And you can do other actions." Ritchie performs the around the world, dog walk, and cradle the baby tricks.

Bobby-Joe is satisfied. "Pretty cool. If you really have too much time on your hands. What about this?" Bobby-Joe points to an old dusty machine.

"That was supposed to be able to tell if someone if lying," Ritchie says.

Bobby-Joe examines the machine. "Did it work?"

"Not enough to use it in a court of law," Ritchie informs him.

Bobby-Joe goes on to another contraption, starts to fiddle with a stereo.

Ritchie smiles. "You like music?"

"Of course," Bobby-Joe says. Ritchie strolls over to a stack of stereo equipment. Pushes buttons.

"How much stuff did your ancestors bring down here?" He asks.

Ritchie tweaks the stereo's EQ. "They thought they might be the last people on Earth, so they brought a whole lot." Ritchie turns to Bobby-Joe. "Wanna see?"

"Am I not seeing now?" Bobby-Joe asks.

"You ain't seen nothing yet," Ritchie sings.

Ritchie hits the play button on the stereo. Blink 182's Dammit begins to play.

Bobby-Joe begins to bob his head to the beat.

Ritchie begins to head bang and motions for Bobby-Joe to follow. Ritchie comes to another set of steel doors.

Bobby-Joe looks unsure, remembers the recent trauma in the elevator.

"This one just opens and closes, no movement," Ritchie assures him.

Bobby-Joe nods.

The two enter an endless warehouse of historical artifacts. Towering shelves filled with items big and small pack the warehouse and go on disappearing into the distance.

Speakers in the warehouse also blast Blink 182. The two head bang and slam dance to the music.

Ritchie holds a hula-hoop up before demonstrating how to use it. Bobby-Joe tries for a second, the hoop dropping quickly. Both men laugh.

Ritchie shows off his small butterfly tattoo on his bicep, while Bobby-Joe reveals his entire back is a tattoo collage of cultural war symbols such as guns, wolves, and bones.

Bobby-Joe disappears behind a shelf and pops back up with post-its all over his face. Ritchie gives him the thumbs up.

"Wheels!" Bobby-Joe exclaims after finding an area of wheeled foot driven vehicles. In moments the two soar through the giant underground warehouse, Ritchie on a skateboard and Bobby-Joe on a scooter. The two fly through the long aisles until Bobby-Joe rides onto a slip and slide and veers out of control, slamming into a decorated Christmas tree.

Blink 182's Dammit ends.

Ritchie helps Bobby-Joe up and the two drag themselves to a nearby work table and chairs.

"That was fun," Ritchie says.

"It was something. This is all something, that is for sure." Bobby-Joe flips through the immense poster collection he's just found. Each is in hard plastic. "So what were posters anyway?"

Ritchie flips through another stack. "They were just big pictures about all types of things."

"What the hell is this?" Bobby-Joe inquires.

Ritchie looks over at it, smiles. "It is a poster of Boy George."

"Boy George?" Bobby-Joe repeats.

Ritchie laughs. "Who knows? A clown? You do know what a clown is?

Don't you?"

"Yes," Bobby-Joe says. "And I agree. He's a clown."

Ritchie thinks for a moment. "There are so many things down here I have not looked at."

Bobby-Joe holds up a poster of Rambo and shows his own muscle.

"He might be slightly bigger," Ritchie teases.

"What about this one?" Ritchie holds up a picture of Michael Jordan flying through the air with his basketball.

The two study the poster for a second.

"Well, isn't it obvious?" Bobby-Joe says.

Ritchie doesn't know.

"He could fly!" Bobby-Joe finishes.

The two ponder it for a moment, until Bobby-Joe spots the poster Ritchie has up. It's Pamela Anderson. "Look at her!"

The two take a look at her long and hard.

"I never saw a young woman in my life," Ritchie says. "Not until I came up to the surface where there I saw two kinds, both off limits to me in some way." He counts on his finger, "The colored women," and touching the second finger, "And the few mindless white women I've encountered." Ritchie shakes his head.

Bobby-Joe slaps Ritchie on his shoulder. "This is no time to be sad. You and I and my people, we are going to start the nation again. There are many young women among my people Ritchie. Women that look much like that right there," Bobby-Joe points to Pamela Anderson.

Ritchie takes another long hard look and imagines. "So you seem very serious about reuniting the states?"

Bobby-Joe pipes up. "Hell yes. It is my sworn oath in life. As well as the sworn oath of hundreds of thousands of people, including high ranking military officials and politicians. In a decade we have united seven states. Since the floods pushed us here we've taken on quite a number of tribes along the way."

Ritchie is silent as he imagines what a new United States would look like. He snaps out of it with the thought of the Colored Empire. "There's a problem."

"Oh?" The warrior looks up to solve problems.

"Something I have not told you."

Bobby-Joe is ready for anything. "A problem? What problem?"

"My people were historians," Ritchie begins, "They taught me the purpose of the United States of America: freedom from oppression."

Bobby-Joe nods. "We have been going by state laws since all our federal buildings were destroyed in the war. But it's basically the same. The US of A is all about unity."

"And if it is your oath to recreate it," Ritchie declares, "then I've got to show you something." He loads up the DVD player onto the giant wall screen.

34

Teecher follows close behind Hunter 311 as the two make their way through the ghettos of Cretaceous Park. The old Hunter keeps his handgun firmly into the young man's back.

"Keep walking!" Teecher shoves him forward.

"Where are we going?" Hunter 311 asks.

"You are going to take me to the other cave," Teecher orders. "Don't turn around, just lead."

"How do you know about it?" Hunter 311 doesn't understand.

"I have known of its existence for years now," Teecher chuckles evilly. "It is just that no one has known its location. It was a bit of a fail-safe at the beginning of our Empire."

"What are you going to do?" Hunter 311 asks him.

"Destroy it you little idiot," Teecher hisses. He shoves the barrel into his back. "Now move faster!"

35

Ritchie shuts off the DVD-R Player, the bloody ending frame disappears from the screen. "So now you have seen first-hand what they do and believe."

Bobby-Joe stews on the couch. He is still taking in what he just saw. Finally, he says, "And you recorded those yourself?"

"Yes," Ritchie answers, he lowers his head in shame. "I just watched for a while. But I couldn't anymore." He looks at Bobby-Joe. "So I decided to do something about it."

The warrior is interested. "What?"

Ritchie gives a stolid look. "I've killed most all of their warriors."

Bobby-Joe is surprised. "When? How many?"

"Today. Over twenty."

"You killed over twenty men today? By yourself, and on their own ground I take it?"

Ritchie nods. "Yes, I did."

Bobby-Joe looks back to the screen frozen on an image of a white that was hunted and killed.

"I recognize those people, at least their clothing," Bobby Joe informs Ritchie.

"You do?"

"A Missouri tribe we encountered a week or so back. It seemed they have a lot of weird cultural customs, one of which is to banish their criminals, elderly, and those deemed useless to the tribe."

"That's why they kept randomly showing up." Ritchie ponders aloud. "I wonder how many they killed."

"I can't believe a society started out like that," Bobby-Joe grimaces. "The Nebraskans are mostly white, but all 7-States have many races."

Ritchie beams. "That's great. Because that is what America was and should be again."

"To the cause!" Bobby-Joe salutes an invisible flag.

Ritchie becomes very serious. "My point is we cannot have this type of thinking in the new found country. Especially if we have the power to prevent it!"

Bobby-Joe thinks. "I agree. So what do we do?"

Ritchie's eyes widen. "They have no place in the US of A Bobby-Joe. No place."

Bobby-Joe understands. "I need to report back with all this."

"Now?" Ritchie asks.

"I am to return upon finding any significant life or information," Bobby-Joe looks serious. "I think this counts."

"Let me grab some food and water," Ritchie replies.

"We won't be walking for long. I can radio a courier once above ground."

Ritchie nods.

"What is that?" Bobby-Joe asks looking up.

"What?" Ritchie looks up as well. "Oh, the hive."

On the ceiling is a giant glass enclosure of a giant bee's nest. Billions of bees swarm around their nest.

"I thought the constant hum down here was just from the computers and generators, but I hear part of it is their buzzing!" Bobby-Joe peers up at them, amazed. "What sort of insect are they?"

Ritchie smiles. "They are bees."

"Bees?" Bobby-Joe says aloud.

"They make the most tasty substance called honey."

"Tasty?" Bobby-Joe almost gags. "You eat from these insects?"

Ritchie laughs hard. "Yes, they make one of the most sweetest foods on the planet."

Bobby-Joe looks away. "Your ancestor's must of really liked the stuff to take them down here and let them thrive like this."

Ritchie nods and bites his lip. "There was another reason actually. I been meaning to ask what the gardening was like back West where you came from."

"Gardening?" Bobby-Joe's eyebrow raises. "Not much at all. Mutated corn could grow here and there. But our society and those we have witnessed since uniting the tribes maintain eating mostly meat."

"There is a reason for that and I think I can fix the outdoor growing problem," Ritchie claims.

"How?" Bobby-Joe demands.

Ritchie points up at the ceiling. "Them."

Bobby-Joe doubts him. "These insects?"

"Bees," Ritchie says.

"Yes, how can bees do that?"

"Bees pollinate flowers and are essential to Earth's homeostasis."

Bobby-Joe cannot believe it. "These bees make fruits and vegetables flower?"

"Many flowers, those flowers in turn create oxygen that feeds humans and animals, who create carbon dioxide plants live on. Take away one variable and the system falls apart. It was theorized that the planet itself would die within a week if bees disappeared from the planet. The bomb seemed to have killed the ones off on this continent at least."

"So if you were to let them go free–"

"I theorize that within a few months vegetation growth would increase exponentially and the Earth's soil would become fertile once again."

"Well, let them out then!"

"I will. Radiation readings show that the atmosphere will level out to an optimal radiation level for them to thrive sometime this week."

"That is good to hear," Bobby-Joe concludes.

"Ya," Ritchie stares up at them for a second, before turning toward the exit. "I am ready then."

The two make their way back to the elevator. Bobby-Joe looks at the sliding metal doors like an enemy.

Ritchie activates the call button. "You can do it. Just remember there is no danger."

The doors open and the giant warrior steps in. He takes the ride up much better the ride down.

36

"Hell yes I want them there!" General Keller yells into a tacky cell phone before ending the call. His entourage surrounds him inside the General's giant military tent in the center of the 7-State Army encampment.

"Open that window!" The General orders as he grabs his oxygen generator and takes a huge huff.

Two soldiers rush to the large tent flap window, releasing it, the bright orange sunbeams fill the tent.

General Keller turns to the window. "Gets hot in here instantly!" General Keller scoffs. "Even worse than our Northwest weather isn't it men?"

The soldiers all answer with a "yes sir."

The General turns to the entourage. "Do you know there was a time those rays were yellow and light, blue skies as far as the eyes can see, and the air whipped around you every so lightly in a way to cool you off while giving you life with oxygen?" He looks at his men. "I sound like a fucking pansy poet, don't I?"

The men do not know what to say.

"That is what tales of old do to men like me. Leaders of men." He approaches the window, feeling the heat on his face. "We yearn for a better life, perhaps due to how short life is, even the healthiest ones. But no matter what we tell ourselves we cannot settle, we know life was better before and can get better again. This may be our curse, our original sin. Our attempt to get back to the garden, to paradise."

The General closes the flap. His men let out a sigh of relief, sweat already pouring from their brows.

A soldier enters and salutes the high ranking officers within the room and waits to speak.

"What is it?" General Keller asks.

"Message in that Sgt. Phillips is on his way back," the soldier announces.

The old General scowls. "Already?" He thinks for a second before his scowl turns to joy. "By God, Bobby-Joe has come through again! Porter, get my truck ready, I want to go pick him up."

"Yes sir," Porter, an officer in the group, replies and exits.

"One more thing sir," the messenger speaks up.

"What is it?" General Keller demands.

"Sgt. Phillips is not alone. There is someone with him."

General Keller lights up even more. "Hot damn!" He looks around at the others. "After months of slowly making our way across this God forsaken land, we have finally found people!"

"But sir," the messenger interrupts, "Sgt. Phillips reported finding only one person."

General Keller approaches the timid soldier, he shutters ever so slightly as his General lays his hand on his shoulder. "With one man you will find more, son." The old General then turns to his entourage once again. "Let's go!"

37

Ritchie and Bobby-Joe traverse another of the countless hills of the Georgian plains.

"Copy," Bobby-Joe says into his radio. "We should be seeing you in the next 30 seconds." He puts the receiver away.

"Who are meeting?" Ritchie asks.

Bobby-Joe smiles. "We are being picked up by the face of the 7-State Army and the last good chance of reuniting the US of A. General Walter Randolph Keller."

"Very distinguished and American name," Ritchie quips.

Bobby-Joe is confused, but something else catches his attention. He looks out onto the horizon and listens intently.

"I hear it too, an engine." Ritchie peers out as well.

Suddenly a military truck soars over a distant hill toward them. General Keller sits in the passenger seat, a few of his entourage with him. Several other combat vehicles jut over the hill after the General.

Ritchie's eyes widen. "What an entrance!"

"Something he is famous for." Bobby-Joe signals to the truck and it veers toward them.

The General's truck pulls up to them.

Bobby-Joe stands and salutes. The entourage salutes back. Ritchie stares for a second before realizing and does his best salute motion. Finally the General salutes back.

"Didn't expect to see you so soon Sergeant!" The General lights a cigar.

"Yes sir, General," Bobby-Joe answers. "After the long haul of deserted land since North Missouri I didn't expect to find anyone this far South."

"Yes," General Keller says eyeing Ritchie. His entourage does as well. "What is your name son?"

"Ritchie, General sir," he tries to sound military. "Ritchie Budushki."

235

"Get in, you two," the General orders. Two of his entourage exit the truck and get in one of the other vehicles.

Bobby-Joe and Ritchie climb in the back seats of the truck and the group of vehicles turn around and head back toward 7-State Army camp.

"Budushki?" The General yells over the wind and loud engine. "You're Russian decent eh?"

"Yes sir," Ritchie blurts, "Pretty much full blooded."

General Keller nods. "Despite the name, I myself am mostly of Russian decent, Crimea area if you know where that was."

"I do," Ritchie admits. "Ukrainian peninsula."

The General is impressed. "And your family name, it has a specific meaning."

Ritchie feels uneasy for some reason. "It does. Are you fluent in Russian, General?"

"No, not really. My mother would speak it now and then is all. But, your name in particular has come up in my past readings of Russian authors."

Bobby-Joe looks at Ritchie as if to say, "I told you he's the real deal."

"You know it as well?" General Keller eyes Ritchie through the rear view mirror.

Ritchie seems forced, answers lowly. "It means the future."

General Keller bellows a laugh. "Oh, how I wish we had some vodka! Yes, it means the future!" The General turns around to face Ritchie. "Are you the future young man?"

"What-" Ritchie begins to question, "I don't know what you mean."

"Well, we have not seen life for hundreds upon hundreds of square miles, our scientists have been saying we just crossed one of the largest areas of destruction of the Great Wars, we began to think we may be the only people left all the way to the East coast, and suddenly we find you. So my question is are you the future?"

Ritchie looks back at the General seriously. "Perhaps I am at least an important factor in the future."

"What sort of factor?" The General asks.

"I think your scout Sgt. Phillips should officially tell you what he has found in and with me."

General Keller's eye narrow at Ritchie, then he locks eyes on Bobby-Joe.

38

"And you saw him dead?" Pupil 316's eyes are wide with dread.

The Pupils all surround Pupil 315 as he starts to tell them the story for the fifth time. "Yes, he was," but then stops, and says, "Look, no, I am not going to tell you again. You just need to realize that something very bad is going on."

The young group emanates fear and shock.

Pupil 315 looks out the dormatory windows. "I don't know what it is exactly, but it is something very bad."

39

The military truck pulls into the 7 State Army encampment. Thousands of soldiers flock to stare at the General, Bobby-Joe, and the first human found in longer than most can remember.

The men make their way to the main military tent by way of a barricaded path. Soldiers salute, give shout outs, and try and touch the General and his entourage as they pass. Just before he enters the tent General Keller turns back to the soldiers and throws food, cigarettes, and small bottles of alcohol to the masses.

They scamper for the goods and cheer on their leader as he disappears through the doorway flaps.

"White Hunters? Sergeant Phillips, you sure this boy is alright?" General Keller studies Ritchie again.

"Yes General," Bobby Joe reveals a tape from his jacket. "I not only observed multiple killings on video, but brought the tape as well, so you could view it."

The General seems outraged, swipes the tape from Bobby-Joe and hands it off to an officer.

The recorded killings begin to play over the large screen in the military tent.

The men in the room become frozen at the images on the screen.

General Keller's mouth drops open, Bobby-Joe grimaces as he watches it for the second time. Yet, Ritchie has seen it enough, seen it first hand, and turns away. Something catches his eye outside the tent, a large group of women walking together. He is mesmerized and seems to float off in a daydream as the women pass.

The video ends and the screen is dark again. The General and his entourage are speechless at first.

"And a settlement is based on this belief?" General Keller asks, seemingly still unable to believe it.

"Yes," Bobby-Joe answers, "And it is more like an Empire than a settlement General."

General Keller turns away in thought. Visions of battles, men fighting men, blood, gunshots, explosions.

"But there is very positive strategic news General," Bobby-Joe goes on.

"Yes?" The General pipes up.

"Ritchie has killed all but a few of their soldiers, the hunter, today in fact."

The General scopes the room for Ritchie. "Ritchie!" He sees him at the window and makes a B-line for him. "The future! You are the future!"

Ritchie doesn't know what to do, seems almost caught, as the old General puts his beefy old arm around him.

"Boy you can't always judge a book by its cover," General Keller bellows. "At least with you. How many of them did you kill?"

Ritchie doesn't answer.

"At least 30 General," Bobby-Joe answers for him.

"So what do you think we should do now?" The General asks.

Ritchie wrist-watch alarm goes off. "I could set off the bombs I planted in the city."

General Keller is in love. "Ritchie," he says, holding his arms out for an embrace.

"Yes sir?" Ritchie is forced to reply.

"I just want to show you my appreciation."

"Just telling me I can set them off is reward enough," Ritchie comments.

General Keller retracts his arms. "Alright son. You have my permission."

Ritchie smiles finally, pushes a combination of buttons on his watch, then looks back up and says, "I love fireworks."

VIII

The Cleansing

1

A huge explosion rattles the city. Chaos rules in downtown Colored Empire. Several buildings explode, sending fire and debris everywhere.

King Amses watches buildings all over his city burn from his balcony. He screams at his entourage. "Call the citizens to help qualm the fire!"

A guard steps forward. "Yes sir!" He answers his King before leaving to carry out the task.

King Amses feels sick. "I cannot just stand here and watch this!" He says to himself. The King stomps back into his chamber. "I'm going to find the men who call themselves politicians around here."

The King's entourage follows him out the chamber entrance.

2

The Pupils in the dormitory look over and see the many explosions from their huge glass windows.

3

"And I can imagine my dress!" Monique exclaims. "It will definitely have to be–"

One of Ritchie's bombs explodes through Crystal's apartment building.

The air conditioning unit hanging above Monique jars free from the wall and slams onto her head, her body disappearing completely under the crushing machine. The explosions send the other girls from the couch, Crystal into a side table and Cicily onto the floor.

The two women lay on the floor for a few moments, yet additional explosions wake Cicily. She shakes her head, looking around, sees the air conditioner where Monique sat and the pooling blood that was oozing from under the machinery.

"Crystal!" Cicily calls out, suddenly looking for her best friend. She spots her lying near the side table. A huge gash on her forehead bleeds steadily. "Crystal!" Cicily calls out again, rushing to her and rolling her over. She then looks before grabbing a scarf nearby and pressing it on Crystal's bleeding forehead.

"We got to get out of here," Cicily declares as she pulls her best friend up to her feet.

Crystal begins to come to, but is still very drowsy. "What happened?"

"I think that white man is attacking the city." Cicily helps her to the front door, but it does not open automatically for them. "Let us out of here," Cicily orders Crystal.

Crystal swings her head around and presses on the digital pad, a number pad appears and she types in four numbers.

The door slides open finally. A scorching fire ensues to the left of the entrance way.

"Are you ready?" Cicily asks Crystal.

Crystal nods.

Cicily helps her best friend out the doorway and to the right to avoid the flames.

4

Hunter 311 and Teecher jump from the explosions.

"What in Deshawn's name is going on?" Hunter 311 asks.

"What do you think?" Teecher snaps. "You've caused all this. By betraying your people and bringing that white into our city!"

"We were both getting chased by the guy only hours ago," Hunter 311 pleas. "I think this was inevitable."

"Shut up!" Teecher demands. "How much further?"

"Not far now," Hunter 311 says. "Under the housing beyond the sacred cave."

"Good," Teecher shoves the gun further into Hunter 311's back. "Faster."

"Right there," Hunter 311 spots the apartment they ended up exiting from after Ritchie was dressed in the White Hunter disguise.

"This place?" Teecher looks unsure.

"This is it," Hunter 311 says. He motions Teecher to enter. "After you."

Teecher smiles. "Funny," he pushes him through the door.

Inside is a bare apartment.

"Where are the occupants?" Teecher asks.

"I don't know," Hunter 311 replies. "No one was here before either."

"Now where?" Teecher asks impatiently.

"In the basement," Hunter 311 tells him.

"Go," Teecher orders.

Hunter 311 opens a door and leads him down the basement steps. They come to a large dark basement, Hunter 311 flips a switch. A bright light reveals a recently dug hole into the basement floor.

"How did he figure it out?" Teecher almost asks himself.

Hunter 311 shrugs. "Are you ready to see the truth?"

"Yeah, whatever," Teecher kicks Hunter 311 into the hole. Then drops down with him.

A small hole has been chipped away in the rock. Teecher turns on his arm flashlight, so does Hunter 311.

"This is the entrance to the cave," Hunter 311 says as he begins climbing through the hole.

"Wait!" Teecher orders him to stay.

Hunter 311 takes his opportunity and disappears through the hole.

Teecher shoots at him, missing. He screams in frustration. "You slippery little bastard!" Teecher slips through the hole after Hunter 311.

5

"Are you hurt?" Demetrious asks Tysheka as he helps her up.

She brushes herself off. "No, I'm fine. What was that?"

"More explosions. Bigger ones." He suddenly thinks of his family and darts out the door.

"More explosions?" Tysheka asks herself before following Demetrious as he charges into the living room.

"I told you all!" The boy cries as he soars into the family room.

The explosion has scattered his family about the living quarters.

"Is everyone alright?" He calls out to his family.

6

Hunter 311 realizes the explosions in the city have shook the surrounding Earth so much that caves are full of dust. He turns off his flashlight and hides from Teecher. He finds a nook to crouch down into and peers through the dust to see.

Suddenly, Teecher appears, grabbing, and dragging him to his feet. "Get up you bitch!" Teecher screams at Hunter 311, then punches him in the gut, completely wilting him. "We are going to make you tough somehow, you little runt!" Teecher lifts his student's face up and sends an uppercut into his chin.

The blow knocks the young Hunter on his behind. Hunter 311 seems not to fight back. Another blow whips his head back. He speaks through blood and spit. "Why do you cover up the truth and promote–" He motions to the Hunter 311 patch on his shoulder. "–lies and death?"

Teecher shakes his head in disgust. "You should have been weeded out from the Academy long ago. You white loving mule!""

Hunter 311 shakes his head. "Why do you hate them so much?"

Teecher screams, "They oppressed us! They committed heinous acts for hundreds of years around the globe!"

Hunter 311 rises, almost calm now. "Those people you are referring to are dead. We have seen nothing that says the whites we are encountering are like them."

Teecher shows a slight sign of fear. "It doesn't matter. They are all the same. It is in their blood!" Teecher turns away from Hunter. "I am sorry it has come to this. But, I should of terminated you when you refused your first kill."

Teecher activates his claw weapon. With a hum his arm grows into the traditional crane-like weapon of the White Hunter.

Hunter 311 activates his claw arm for the first time as a Hunter. He watches it grow and turns into fighting stance.

Teecher grins and attacks, swinging his arm at Hunter 311. The claw's talons barely scratch Hunter 311's chest.

The young Hunter looks at his wound. Teecher throws a backhand swipe at him, but this time he is ready and is already out of the way.

Hunter 311 feels confident suddenly. "Teaching and fighting are two different things I'm afraid."

Teecher smirks at the insult. "You finally grew some did you?" Teecher laughs and strikes from above.

Hunter 311 halts the attack with his own claw, holding Teecher's talons right before his eyes. The claw fingers clamp together in anticipation. With all of his might, Hunter 311 pushes his ex-teachers claw-weapon away. He kicks the old Hunter in his gut sending him backward.

Teecher is enraged. He rushes back to Hunter 311 spearing him into the ground. With inhuman speed, Teecher rises above the young Hunter and steps on his shoulder.

"You have put up a better fight than I expected," Teecher seethes. "I am proud of you for that."

Teecher wraps his claw-hand around his torso. Hunter 311 screams in pain.

"You have turned against your own people," Teecher declares as he keeps Hunter 311 pinned. "You are a traitor." Teecher begins crushing Hunter 311's ribs. "And will likely be buried in this cave forever."

Hunter 311 screams. He grits through the pain, "Just because I believe a person should be judged by the actions and not how they were born, does not make me a traitor to my people!" "Whether it is today or not, young Hunter 311," Teecher announces. "You should come to realize that in this world it is white versus black! You must choose! And to choose anything but black is to deny yourself!"

"You," Hunter grunts, "Need to realize that sometimes things are not just black and white. Hunter 311 finishes, "Sometimes, things are just gray!"

A mechanical rip! Teecher is almost pale, stares forward for a moment, then down to see his own mechanical arm has been torn from his body. A bone can be seen where his real arm once existed. Blood spurts from the stump. Teecher screams in agony.

Hunter 311 rises, holding the claw-arm of his one-time teacher. He bashes the arm on the ground and throws the heavy steel contraption thirty feet.

Teecher falls backward now in shock.

Hunter 311 seizes him by the torso now and bashes him against the cave wall three times before letting his lifeless body fall to the cave floor. Hunter 311 studies his body for a moment, spying the missing arm and bloody mush where Teecher's head once was. Then, he collapses against the cave wall and sits down, exhausted, his head falling between his knees.

Suddenly, his radio beeps, signaling an incoming call. Ritchie's voice crackles through." Rookie! You there?"

Hunter 311 listens for a second, still not moving.

Ritchie's voice comes through again. "If you are there, pick up!"

Hunter 311 gets up finally and snatches up the radio. "I'm here," he returns.

Ritchie does a yahoo. "You made it partner! How did you manage getting by your mean old teacher?"

Hunter 311 shoots a look at the severed claw arm not far away. "I took something he really needed."

Ritchie laughs. "Good. I'm glad the student finally conquered the teacher." Awkward silence.

"Listen, brother," Ritchie begins to speak with urgency now. "Something is about to happen, and I need you to do something extremely vital for your people as well as mine."

7

"Even after my, my house getting blasted, my mom's face getting smashed up, and my whole array of brothers and sisters being traumatized, my family is still in the dark!" Demetrious says as he paces back and forth in his room.

Tysheka watches him for a while before speaking. Finally, she speaks, "So let's go find out what is going on."

Demetrious stops in his tracks, seems truly intrigued by the idea. "Yes, I mean it seems staying inside buildings is the wrong thing to do when it comes to these explosions."

Just then, the giant screen in the room turns on, an image of the Man with the Microphone appears.

"Attention all citizens! Get ready for an important announcement." The Man with the Microphone announces. "Presenting the King!"

The camera turns to the King now. He is not in his usual relaxed mood, instead a fidgety and fearful man stands before the camera. He gathers his thoughts, not sure how to start, finally he speaks. "A situation has occurred," he shifts his weight. "We are under attack. At this point we do not know the who exactly is behind the attacks. Therefore, I have decided to institute a draft. All men and women 14-years and older are to report to the Academy immediately. All children are to go to the Capital Building." The King walks off camera.

Demetrious smiles. "It looks like we must leave after all." He grabs his backpack and opens the door for Tysheka.

In the living room Demetrious' family is in disarray. They all still watch the living room screen, yet voiced shoot back and forth. The camera swings back to the Man in the Microphone. "Everyone stay calm, and do what your King has ordered immediately."

8

The screen inside the Pupil dormitory shuts off.

"I thought that TV was broken," Pupil 318 comments. "Why don't we ever watch it?

"Because it is for emergency use only kid," Hunter 315 informs him. "It has never been on the entire time I have lived here. Ten years now."

The Pupils all seem to think about it for a moment.

"So you heard the King," Pupil 318 announces. "You guys need to pack light and head out."

The other Pupils look at him in shock.

"You are too old," Pupil 316 stands up and begins to approach Pupil 318.

"Stay where you are brainiac." Pupil 318 orders. He turns to the dorm windows and peers onto the chaotic city. "When times end, they end like this."

"Only hours ago the city was fine, in peace, happy," Pupil 317 begins to cry.

Pupil 315 turns to him in disgust. "Stay strong, boy!"

Pupil 317 tries to muffle his cries and wipes his eyes.

"You need to take care of your brother here," the Pupil 315 orders the other twin. "And all of you need to be out of here now!"

9

Hunter 311 spots Demetrious' large apartment. He quickly approaches the front door and rings the bell. After a moment, the quirky father opens the door in his ever present lab coat. "Hello, may I help," he begins, but stops in mid-sentence when he observes Hunter 311's attire, tainted with dirt and blood.

"Hello, Mr. Jones," Hunter 311 says, "I am looking for my niece Tysheka."

'Of course," Ms. Jones says with a sign of relief. "I found out just today that you are Tysheka's uncle. Just made the Hunting ranks and all."

"Yes, sir, I don't mean to be rude, but it is an emergency, I need to talk to my niece."

"Emergency?" The man has never heard the word. "What is that?"

Hunter 311 shakes his head, doesn't have time for this. "I do apologize," he passes Mr. Jones, "Demetrious' room please?"

"Down the hall, last on the left," he answers.

Hunter 311 hops into the house vestibule.

The family sits hovering together in the living room as if waiting for something, all of them holding a single traveling bag. Half of the outer wall of their house has fallen through.

Hunter 311 feels a sudden sharp awkwardness. Although everything is falling apart, he suddenly remembers he is an agent of the government, a symbol of it. And the destruction ensuing in the city, on these people and their home, is greatly his fault, at least partly.

Mr. Jones begins to ramble. "Does this have to do with the explosions we heard earlier? I keep telling the family the government is probably doing some work somewhere or mining. I mean most people don't even know what an explosion is, but with my past experience with working in the government mines

I know what the sound is. But, Demetrious is all shook up about them."

Hunter 311 does not answer him. He spots the hallway, holds his hand out, "May I?"

"Well, yes, but they are gone," Mr. Jones says finally.

"Gone where?" Hunter 311 demands.

"Haven't you heard the King's declaration? All children were reported to go to the Capital Building. All adults, well everyone 14-years and older, must report to the Academy for the draft."

Hunter 311 shakes his head.

"I wanted for all of us to go together, but they insisted on leaving right away." Mr. Jones turns to his family in the living room. "We are about to leave now, I just had a few things to finish in the lab."

Mr. Jones turns back, but Hunter 311 has already disappeared out the front door. He sighs, shrugs, looks at his mute and waiting family before sulking back into the door leading to his lab.

10

King Amses marches toward the Academy, his entourage on his heels.

"This draft, my King," the head advisor asks, "How will we train the citizens?"

King Amses waves his advisor's question away. "Well, the White Hunters will of course. Have you reached the fleet via radio yet?"

The advisor looks to another in the group, he shakes his head. "Not yet, my King."

The King looks out into the horizon, "I wonder where they are? Are communications down?"

The advisor looks to the same man again, he again shakes his head.

"No, my King, the communications lines are working."

11

Bobby-Joe stands outside his officer's tent, running his finger over the material of the door flap. The machine-made from 20th century, a true survivor, a remnant of the military that once ruled the land. He had never seen anything like it when it was issued to him. His homes were always made of animal hides, or pieces of various material once he left home.

"Is that you Bobby?" His wife calls out.

Bobby-Joe opens the tent door. "Yes, my dear."

His wife stands with their newborn at her breast. "Well, come in and tell me what in Earth is going on here!"

Bobby-Joe reluctantly steps in. He gazes around his illustrious home. Handcrafted bed and furniture, including table and a set of living room couches, silverware from the 19th and 20th centuries, food lying in wait. And a beautiful new family. He has everything he ever wanted, coming from a destitute and broken home. So why does he feel this way about what he is about to be a major part of?

"What's wrong honey?" His wife can tell already.

"We have found a white as I already have told you," Bobby-Joe begins.

"Yes," she nods in wait.

"Well, we have also found a new society."

"That is great!" The wife says enthusiastically. But, she notices her husband seems even more distraught with her reaction. "What is it?"

"They are not a good society, my love." He turns away from her.

"Will we have war with them?" She adjusts the infant.

Bobby-Joe nods. "I reckon something worse than war."

"Worse than war?"

12

Cicily rests Crystal down onto a city bench. "Not far now to the hospital." She sits next to her friend. "You didn't fall asleep did you? That's why I've been carrying you the last block?"

Cicily touches Crystal's hair, and realizes she is gone when she looks into her lifeless eyes. She closes them, then stares out into the burning city.

A man passing by stops before them. "She is gone. You need to go on without her."

Cicily looks up at him. "To where?"

"The King has ordered all over 14-years old to go to the Hunter Academy." He gives her one last look before going on to where his King ordered him to go.

Cicily thinks about Tysheka, just 13-years old, must be safe from the draft. It was her brother she would be with now.

Cicily rests Crystal's body, propping her up almost as if she still was living, before trekking toward the place that held her brother captive from her growing up, the power that prevented her from ever getting to know him or getting close to him, this place of power was the Hunter Academy.

13

"And because they believe this, practice this, the consensus is to kill them all?"

"Not the children," Bobby-Joe blurts.

"And how would you guarantee no children are hurt during such an act of violence?" His wife holds their baby closer.

"We already have someone inside handling that." Bobby-Joe approaches her face-to-face now. "This is the only way. And it is beyond our control." He touches his infant son's forehead.

His wife nods in understanding.

14

Hunter 311 soars up the steps of the Capital Building. He enters the rotunda to find masses of children have already gathered.

"Tysheka!" He looks around, swarmed by little ones. Many approach the Hunter in awe, asking questions and requesting signatures.

Hunter 311 pushes past the children, "Tysheka! Demetrious!" He continues to scan the large group children.

"Uncle," Tysheka's voice finally rings out. She has just entered the Capital Building rotunda, Demetrious right behind.

"Tysheka!" Hunter 311 calls back. The two rush through the crowd to meet and hug.

"What is going on Uncle?"

Hunter 311 does not know how to answer. "Look, sweety. Our people are in a lot of trouble." He looks at Demetrious, who stands listening intently.

"Trouble?" Tysheka asks.

Hunter 311 looks around at the children now. Many have quieted talking to each other and are listening to the Hunter.

"Hello!" A child's voice calls out.

The children all turn to see the Pupils under the age cutoff entering the rotunda.

Pupil 316 spots Hunter 311. "Hello sir!" He says.

"Have you seen Pupil 315?" Hunter 311 asks him.

"He is too old to come," Pupil 316 answers. "He was going to go to the Academy courtyard with the adults."

"We tried to stop him, but we couldn't," little Hunter 318 speaks up at Hunter 311.

Hunter 311 stoops down and embraces him for a second. "It is OK. He wouldn't have come here for anything in the world."

"I wanted to go with him and see my parents," Hunter 318 whines.

Hunter 311 gives him another squeeze. "I know little one. But, you must be strong." He rises and looks out onto the sea of children that will secure the future of his people.

"We need your help. Because there is trouble." Hunter 311 speaks louder to address everyone, "All of you. The future of the Colored lies within all of you. But as I said, you must remain strong, and do exactly what I say."

The children group together and face Hunter 311. He begins to look at the children's countless faces. Faces of fear, or misunderstanding, or sadness. Innocent faces that constitute the future of the citizens of the Colored Empire.

Hunter 311 continues to speak. "Can you be strong for your people?"

15

The adults of the Colored Empire are gathered in the large courtyard of the Hunter Academy. Shouts of fear and distress emanate from the crowd.

Several groups of men are irate. One group starts to yell together in protest. Another begins to fight among themselves.

Several fires burn bright within the city, a few so close the courtyard is getting hotter by the minute.

The Man with the Microphone appears from Hunter Academy entrance doors. The crowd boos upon seeing him.

"Calm down brothers and sisters," the Man with the Microphone says. "We must stay strong through this!"

The crowd boos louder.

"We don't want to hear it! Turn your microphone off!" One woman screams.

The crowd roars in agreement.

"The city is burning to the ground!" A man yells.

Three men run up the stairs and grab the Man with the Microphone.

"Oh no," he says almost robotically.

The men begin to hit him on top of the head. The largest man raises his arm again to strike, but a single drop of rain hits his forearm and he freezes.

More drops. More. And suddenly a down pours ensues upon the city.

"It is a miracle from Godallah!" the Man with the Microphone screams into his precious tool he held onto during the brief beating. He jumps up into one of his dances.

"It is a miracle!" The King's voice booms through the Hunter Academy loudspeakers. "The city is saved. Look, even now the fires are going out!"

The King and his entourage appear on the steps with the Man with the Microphone. The men who had beaten the media star flee back into the crowd.

The torrential rain beats down upon everyone, even the King. He goes on as if not caring at all. "It is time for change!"

The crowd is baffled with the word.

The Man with the Microphone chimes in to help. "Your King has made some decisions in an attempt to solidify the future of the Colored Empire."

"Why have we been called to the Hunter Academy?" One man yells.

Another citizen screams, "Are you to make us all Hunters?"

The King grabs the microphone from the Man with the Microphone. "No! You are to be soldiers!"

The citizens quiet down now. They do not know what the word means.

The King continues. "A soldier is a man or woman that fights to preserve their land. That is what you will be."

The citizens scream boos again.

Another rash citizen squirms through the masses, almost feet from the King. "Who will teach us to be soldiers?"

"Our great White Hunters of course," the King replies into the microphone.

16

The Hunter Academy building stands wide and strong, with its granite foundation and smooth architecture. Although not as tall as the Capitol Building nor the King's castle, the breadth of the building shows a timeless opulence among the other city structures.

Hunter 311 soars back up the steps and through the main doors and down the sacred hallway. He notices right away the Academy is still empty, giving him the same eerie feeling he had sneaking in earlier. Usually every inch of the Academy would be bustling with Hunters, Pupils, and other staff.

Only the detailed photos of the past Head Hunters stare him down as he speeds toward his goal. Each picture shows the historical trajectory of Hunter weaponry and culture. From the first more primitively weaponized Hunters armed with the katana and revolver, to the more modern Hunters who gained technological advances such as the claw arm and laser guns.

Each past Head White Hunter eye him as if they know what he is about to do, and as much as their dead souls and lifeless pictures can, they seem to possess an urge and an afterlife wish to strike Hunter 311 dead.

Hunter 311 stops at two sets of great doors lying in the middle of the sacred hallway. A huge plaque on the doors to the East reads, "School and Training Rooms," while the Western doors' sign is much smaller and reads, "Residences."

Hunter 311 reveals two bombs from his pack, holding each up towards the two sets of doors.

17

The children of the Colored Empire reach the outskirts of the city.

"Here we are," Demetrious states. He looks back at the Colored Empire. The fires in the city seem to have increased.

One child starts to cry out loud.

Tysheka spots him. "Sam?" She approaches him. "Sam, it's all right."

"You know him?" Demetrious asks.

"Yes, his uncle is my uncle's teacher at the Academy. He lives not far from me too." Tysheka kneels down to him. "It is OK, you will see your momma again."

Sam shakes his head.

"Why?" Tysheka asks.

"Momma's dead," he says before lowering his head.

"The explosions?" Demetrious asks.

Sam looks up only for a second, then shakes his head "yes."

Tysheka gives him a hug before looking into his eyes. "You will be safe now."

Sam doesn't respond.

Tysheka rises and turns back to the West. "Now we go toward the sunset just as Uncle told us."

"Are you sure?" Demetrious asks. "Your Uncle seemed a little out of it."

Tysheka scowls at him. "You can go back if you want," she motions to the endless line of children behind them. "But I am leading them to safety, just as my Uncle told me to."

Most of the children await with positive attitudes, sheer curiosity of what lies outside a world they have never known. The few that show fear or sadness are being comforted by others.

"Are you ready?" Tysheka calls out to the mass of children.

The group confirms and the children of the Colored Empire leave their city for the first and last time.

18

Hunter 311 reenters the sacred cave.

Teecher's corpse still lies beside the wall. His arm not far away.

Hunter 311 kneels and sets the bomb near his old teacher's body. "You're getting what you wanted after all." He pushes the button on the bomb.

19

King Amses spots Lieutenant Hunter exit the academy. "Speaking of our great White hunters now." The King approaches the Elder Hunter and sees a look of defeat in his face. "What is it?" The King orders.

Lieutenant Hunter shakes his head, "All the Hunters are dead, my King."

The King shows disbelief, then outrage. "Dead? How could this happen? There are over 25 of them!"

"It seems the one white has killed them all," the Lieutenant informs.

The King balls up his fist. "And how do you know this?"

"Well," he can barely look at the King. "He radioed to us."

The King cannot believe it. "And what about the few who were ordered to track and kill hunter 311 within the city?"

Lieutenant cannot help but lower his eyes slightly as he answers. "Missing with no communication sire."

The citizens have heard the discussion. Suddenly, the crowd begins to charge the King and his entourage.

Lieutenant Hunter grabs the King and rushes him into the Academy before shutting the doors on the ensuing crowd. The Senators and Head White Hunters stand inside the Academy entrance hall.

King Amses looks at them with disgust. "You were in here hiding?" The King turns away from them to sit on a bench. "The world is over as we know it!"

Lieutenant Hunter's radio blares, he answers it, listens.

"What is it?" King Amses demands. "It seems the sacred cave has been destroyed," Lieutenant Hunter replies.

Everyone is in dismay.

The Lieutenant listens to his radio still, before placing back in its holder. "The Hunter Academy has been bombed as well."

The radio blares again.

"Answer that and tell me what else has gone wrong!" The King barks.

Lieutenant Hunter answers the radio again, listens. He drops the radio to his side, speechless.

"What? What?" The King shrieks. He jumps from the bench, pushing two of his entourage aside, and grabs the radio. "This is the King," he yells into the radio. "What is it?"

He listens, then his eyes widen. "The children?"

20

West of the Colored Empire, Tysheka leads the massive group of Colored children to an awaiting line of the 7 State Armies.

Many of the children cry in fright at the sight of countless white warriors lined up before them.

Even Demetrious is unsure.

"It is alright," Tysheka tells the quivering children. "We need to go to them."

The children listen and trudge on toward the menacing line of whites. As they near the line women emerge from between the soldiers to compassionately take in the children by whisking them through and behind the line of soldiers.

21

"How can they all be gone?" King Amses is pale, he clutches his chest. The radio buzzes again, he listens. "Where? Right now?"

The King walks over to a window. He spots Hunter 311 walking up the city's main walkway. The young Hunter drags his teacher's severed claw behind him.

"What does this have to do with what is going on?" King Amses asks. "Where is he going?"

Sargent Hunter approaches the window. "He's coming here my King."

The King makes his decision. He immediately grabs three servant girls and proceeds with them past the two groups to the rear of the hall.

"Where are you going King Amses?" Senator Mathis asks.

The King turns back. "You all have to figure this one out. I did nothing to that young Hunter. I'm going through one of the secret royal passages." He pushes onto the molding on the far hallway wall. The wall opens up into a passageway. The King enters the doorway with his small entourage. "Good luck!" He says as the door closes behind him.

Outside, Hunter 311 trudges up the street. The citizens spot him, beaten and bloody, and the amputated mechanical claw arm in his grasp. They forget their onslaught of the Academy, their eyes frozen on Hunter 311.

"This is our chance!" Lieutenant Hunter exclaims.

"What do you mean?" Senator Mathis wants to know.

"The crowd has calmed," Lieutenant Hunter states.

"More like looking for other ways to get in here," Senator Makin speaks up.

"Either way," Lieutenant Hunter announces, "If we live it stands that Teecher must be our scapegoat. Especially given he has killed Teecher."

"All blame will be set on Teecher," Senator Mathis agrees.

22

Ritchie opens another pack and begins to fill it with belongings. He fills it with clothing and grabs a portrait of his family when he was a teen, peering at it momentarily before resting it on top of the clothes and shutting the pack closed. He sets it next to his suitcase filled with technology.

"Now to prepare the data room," Ritchie says to himself as he makes his way out of his room to the other side of the bunker.

He comes to a steel door with a large sign stating simply, "DATA." He opens it and walks through.

Inside is a large room with giant walls of computer memory. The wall is lit up with lights that power and control the massive memory structure.

Ritchie approaches a computer and logs on. He takes the mouse and clicks on the main drive. Inside the tree structure he scrolls down past many folders including agriculture, history, medicine, and stops on war technology.

"Goodbye," Ritchie right clicks the folder and clicks on delete.

"Are you sure you want to delete this folder?" The computer asks. "Folder War Technology, containing four point five million subfolders, 40 trillion files, making 47, 344 Gigabytes? Yes or No?"

Ritchie clicks on yes. The delete bar begins to increase as the files disappear. Ritchie walks out of the data room and heads for the elevator, but stops in his tracks.

"I almost forgot," he walks over to a digital panel on the wall. "Perhaps on purpose." He types in a code and hits enter.

"Initializing release door." The computer's voice announces.

"I cannot keep you for my own!" Richie yells. "You're free!"

The bees see the panel door slide open. Countless yellow bees soar up through the tube toward the surface.

"You're free," he says again, lowly this time, before turning and walking to the elevator. He pushes the elevator button before looking back at the bunker one last time.

Generations upon generations of people were born, lived, and died down here, he thinks to himself. "And I am the last one," he says aloud.

The elevator doors slide open and he gets in. He pushes the button inside and the doors slide shut, he starts to rise.

23

An explosion rips through an Empire gas line, sending a pressurized flame through the underground pipe to an agriculture station outside the city. The station explodes into flames.

24

The elevator stops abruptly, the lights go out.

"What the hell?" Ritchie asks. "The power?" He pulls out a handheld PC.

"Massive destruction to power retrieval center 4 in Southwest sector! Magnetism, solar, and methane retrieval mechanisms 100% destroyed!"

"Switch power to PRC 5 now!" Ritchie yells into the device.

The power returns and the elevator rises again.

25

The data room turns back on. The computer takes several minutes to reboot. Then the deletion process of the war technology folder begins again.

26

Countless soldiers of the 7-State Army await orders West of the Colored Empire. The warriors are visibly eclectic, a combination of ancient and modern military. Some have cars and motorcycles, though many stand alone. Weapons of the soldiers vary from swords, machetes, and axes to pistols and even large projectile weapons. Many have corn, wheat, potatoes, or bear and deer bones and hide perched upon their helmets or embroidered on their uniforms. A group of musicians stand off to the side, guitars, bass, and walking drum sets.

A Jeep pulls up. Inside sits General Keller and three other old men dressed in worn military uniforms with a multitude of medals and accommodations on them. Bobby-Joe and a few other soldiers appear at the vehicle doors.

The old men and Bobby-Joe all draw their blades and kneel in prayer. Every soldier kneels also.

The men pray in unison. "Yea, though I walk through the valley of the shadow of death, I will fear no evil: for thou art with me; thy rod and thy staff they comfort me. Thou preparest a table before me in the presence of mine enemies: thou anointest my head with sword; my cup runneth over. Surely victory and accomplishment shall follow me all the days of my life: and I will dwell in the house of the Lord forever. Amen."

The men stand and turn to the old USA flag. Fifty stars, twenty stripes. The thousands put their hands on their hearts and begin speaking. "I pledge allegiance to the flag of the United States of America, and to the republic for which it stands: one nation under God, indivisible, with liberty and justice for all."

Bobby-Joe turns to General Keller. "The armies are ready for your speech General."

General Keller glances at his counterparts. "We actually thought you should be the one to make the speech today, soldier."

Bobby-Joe looks uneasy.

"After all," the General adds, "It was your exceptional scouting that led to this unfortunate, but necessary step in the restoration of our country."

Bobby-Joe takes a long breath. "Yes sir." The warrior turns to his fellow soldiers. A soldier hands him a microphone. "I am honored to speak to the 7-State Army!"

"Hoo-ah!" 7-State Armies yell in unison.

Bobby-Joe speaks into the microphone. "Our discovery of the one called Ritchie has finally brought us to the end of our quest to find out who we were and who we are."

The masses of soldiers listen intently.

27

Ritchie and the historians and scientists of the 7-States ride the elevator down to his bunker. Ritchie studies the men surrounding him.

The elevator lands and the doors open. The scientists rush into the technological wonderland. Ritchie stays in the elevator. One of the scientists looks back, but the elevator doors have closed.

"Hey look at this!" A scientist yells from the data room. The others rush in.

They observe a computer deleting a folder named war technology, 98% done.

"Stop it!" One scientist cries.

The youngest of them dives onto the abort button, saving 1% of the original folder.

"What is it?" The older scientist shouts.

The younger man opens the folder, one subfolder remains, entitled "atomic."

28

Bobby-Joe goes on. "This man offers to us magnificent technologies and more importantly, an endless archive of human history. It is history that will be the key in the restoration of the US of A!"

"Hoo-ah!" 7-Sate Armies yell in unison.

Bobby-Joe gazes out into the 7-State Army with a solemn look.

"Now each state has been informed about this operation and what we are about to do." Bobby-Joe begins to pace. "Today will be a day each one of you will want to forget for the rest of your lives. But do not let it become a day of infamy for the US of A."

The warrior looks the line up and down as he speaks. "In the sparse history the 7-States have, we are taught an empire once existed very much like the one we are about to face. This empire was called the Nazi Party and it began during what people called the Second World War. Now we don't know if that war was the end war. But we do know that this empire attempted to murder an entire race. Such ideology has no place in the reformation of the US of A. We have the power to make sure history does not repeat itself!"

"Hoo-ah!" 7-State Armies yell in unison.

Bobby-Joe raises his sword and pistol. "Let this battle be the first and last time our new country has to destroy an enemy from within! Let this be the only civil war we will ever have! Let it be the day we solidify what our country will stand for!"

"Hoo-ah!" 7-State Armies yell in unison. The soldiers let out battle cries.

Bobby-Joe turns to his senior officers. The old men motion for him to go on. He nods and begins to lead the army lines forward.

29

Cicily reaches the crowded Academy courtyard. Citizens stand around confused, some fighting amongst each other.

"Cicily!" A female voice calls out to her.

Cicily doesn't recognize the voice, and at first cannot place the face, but it comes to her suddenly. "Shamarra Turner. How are you?"

The woman is distraught, and has obviously been crying. "Besides all this? I can't find my father."

"Oh no," Cicily says. She had been noticing Mr. Turner's erratic behavior as of late.

"We were all wrapped up in the Debate, he must of gone out the door. Tyrone is out looking for him instead of reporting here as the King decreed." Shamarra puts her face in her hands and begins to cry again.

"It's alright," Cicily consoles her. Out of the corner of her eye she spots him walking up the street. Her whole being brightens up. "That's my brother!"

She begins to push her way through the crowd toward him, only quickly calling back to Shamarra Turner. "I am sure you will find him."

30

Pupil 315 peers out of the Academy side exit. From the view he can see the chaotic courtyard. He realizes this is where he should go, his destiny, and takes a large gulp of dry nothing before heading out.

"You have weapons?" A crazed male citizen grabs his arm.

Pupil 315 almost jumps in fright, but instantly punches the man in his jaw, knocking him out cold. The young Pupil looks down at the man for a second before dashing away from the scene.

He jumps the waist-high courtyard barrier to join the chaos of the crowd.

31

The Senators and Head Hunters all signal they are ready before they exit the Academy. Numerous citizens are about to charge the two groups, but stop when they see Hunter 311 approaching.

Hunter 311 enters the courtyard. Citizens make way for him to approach the Academy steps.

Cicily keeps pushing her way through the crowd toward her brother.

Lieutenant Hunter calls out to Hunter 311. "It seems you have been in battle with your Teecher."

Hunter 311 throws the claw-arm before the two groups' feet.

Cicily gasps, then she watches silently.

Some of the Senators look away from the bloody appendage, though the Head Hunters do not flinch.

"He knew just as you did," Hunter 311 grunts. He looks in the eyes of each of these important men. "Why do perpetuate this? What are you scared of?"

Senator Mathis steps forward finally. "There is a reason, my young confused Hunter. Do you not see the destruction only one intelligent white can do?" The old man throws his hands up.

Hunter 311 looks to the destruction for a moment: the fires, the smoke, then begins to speak, "His name is Ritchie. He is a man like you and me. He came up from the ground after living with a group of many races to find himself being hunted by us!"

"What do you plan to do? Why are you in public like this?" Lieutenant Hunter demands.

"If Teecher attacked you and you killed him as the Fair-and-Square Doctrine states, then you will face no charges," Sergeant Hunter adds.

Hunter 311 shakes his head. Turns to the citizens transfixed on him. "I've no desire to perpetuate any more lies."

The Senators and Head White Hunters give looks to each other.

Senator Makin steps forward. "Then what do you want Hunter 311?"

Hunter 311 steps back, addresses all citizens of the Colored Empire. "All should know: There is an army of whites less than a quarter mile from here, perhaps closer."

"You lie!" Senator Mathis contends.

Hunter 311 calls out. "Unfortunately for us all, I am not. Unlike us, they are a people of war. Their males trained to fight from birth, their females stubborn and faithful."

The Senators and White Hunters seem to realize they are doomed.

"This union of peoples is on a mission to reunite the old country this land once was. It was a land based on unity and celebration of racial difference. Ritchie watched us Hunters for weeks, recorded the kills, and presented them to this white army today," Hunter 311 fumes. "What do you think they are going to do?"

No answer.

Chaos breaks out in the courtyard again. Now, as if the realization of their fate, the citizens begin to viciously fight and attack each other, several head immediately for the Senators.

"Now, now, my dear citizens, we need to save this type of energy for protecting ourselves," Senator Mathis pleads.

The Senators and Head Hunters turn and flee up the Academy steps, but the doors will not open.

Hunter 311 looks around. He doesn't see his sister Cicily's freshly lifeless body being trampled by the crowd. "Godallah help us all," he whispers.

32

A huge roar of thousands of screaming men rings out in the Empire. The Colored citizens stop fighting one another and the two groups of elders stand atop the Academy steps frozen with fear.

Bobby-Joe leads the 7-State Army forces into the city. Thousands of huge white warriors flood the unprotected kingdom. The citizens of the Empire seem to watch the swarms as if dreaming.

The white warriors slaughter with speed and accuracy. No Colored citizen even tries to defend themselves.

The Senators flee from the steps, but warriors slay them as they swarm past. The Head Hunters draw their weapons to fight, but the mobs of warriors engulf them.

Pupil 315 watches the white warriors in horror, frozen by the shear idea that what he is seeing is even real. Years of believing whites were extinct, a myth, something to entertain. He was now seeing the reality of it all. Of the world. And what the Empire was hiding after all.

Pupil 315 attempts to draw his student pistol, but a large bald white warrior with a long beard and piercings all over his face and body charges him and knocks him to the ground. "Die!" Is all he hears from the giant warrior before the giant battle axe slams down on his head and crushes his skull.

Ritchie walks among the carnage, watching, but not partaking. He spots Hunter 311 standing among the battle as if he was in the eye of the storm.

The two lock eyes for a moment.

Then Hunter 311 looks into the sky. He seems free finally. He seems to understand and accept. He raises his arms to the sky and is taken away in the warrior horde.

33

Several miles away from the Colored Empire the King emerges from the remnants of an old world water system. He is followed by his female concubines and a young man dressed in workers clothes.

"You are sure they are both completely self sustaining?" The King asks the young worker.

"Yes, my King," the young man reveals a remote from his pocket and punches a sequence of buttons. "We could live in the vehicle or the bunker for as long as we want."

The King smiles. "Excellent."

Suddenly a large recreational vehicle flies up, its doors opening for them. An endless array of solar panels line the entire surface of the vehicle.

"So far I like you much more than your father," the King says before entering the RV, his entourage of women follows him up. The young man looks around before entering as well.

Inside the vehicle lies a garden under high intensity lights, a water catcher, a television, and comfortable seating.

The King turns to him. "Yes, young Harlow I like you much more than your old man. And to show you I am giving you Shondra over there. Besides, we need an extra jump start in getting our race going again."

The young man eyes the young woman happily, yet turns to his King. "But only two men and several women will not create a race. There are many factors that could hinder or halt our lines."

The King rests in the large middle seat. "That is why I have a stash of our people elsewhere."

"Elsewhere?" Young Harlow asks.

"Of course. And only the best." He motions for all of his concubines to come to him, even Shondra for now. "Now drive East, Williams."

34

The two men in white rubber suits pull the old ambulance truck up to the ancient water company. The driver jumps out and gets out his radio.

"We are here, Sire," the man says into the radio, "Don't see ya anywhere."

"I told you we were late!" The other man in white bemoans from the passenger seat.

The driver silences the radio and yells, "Shut up!"

The man in the passenger seat shakes his head.

The radio buzzes and crackles.

"I cannot hear you, Sire," the driver says, "Please say again."

The driver holds the radio up to his ear and listens to crackling words he can barely understand, then the radio suddenly booms King Amses' voice: "Did you complete every task I gave you?"

"Yes, Sire," the driver answers. "We did everything just as you instructed. The gas line gave us just enough time to extract the data. And all the whites have been destroyed as well. Man, there were a bunch of them crazies. The scientists did a number on them. Do you know what one of them–"

"Yes, yes, I know." The King shuts him up. "Are you sure everything was completed?"

"Yes, we are sure, I have the list right here," the driver begins to search his pockets.

The radio crackles the King again. "We can go over the list later. Job well done boys."

The driver stops searching and smiles from his King's favor. "What now Sire?" The driver radios.

"We stick to the plan he created. See the old road East. Take it. We are only a few minutes ahead of you." The radio buzzes out.

"Yes Sire!" He answers excitedly into the radio before putting back on his belt.

"What did the King say?" The man in the passenger seat yells from the truck.

"He said we just missed him!" The man jumps back in the driver's seat.

"How long ago?"

"Maybe fifteen minutes," the driver puts the truck in drive, "We need to drive East he says."

"East?" The man in the passenger seat repeats.

"Yes, East."

"The Engineer was right all along, wasn't he?" The passenger man asks.

"Well, obviously."

"Did you mention that we took a few knick-knacks as well?" The man flips through a Penthouse magazine.

"Not yet. We will show him everything we got." The driver practices his yo-yo wrist flip, the yo-yo spinning down, and then back up into his hand. "I finally did it!"

"Well, I guess you were right. That's what it does," the man in the passenger seat pushes the power button on the boom box resting on the truck floor. Blink 182's Dammit begins to play.

The truck peels off into the distance.

35

Several of the bees from Ritchie's bunker fly past some gnarled trees. One bee breaks away from the small swarm and lands on a branch. He crawls up the dark bark, around the tree to a lone bloomed flower. The bee climbs onto the flower and begins his work.

On the bottom of the same branch a butterfly breaks free from its cocoon.

36

The old woman once called Tysheka sits in her rocking chair surrounded by her 76 grandchildren. She smiles and holds up the children's classic, "The Tortoise and the Hare."

Tyrone, a grandchild of 5-years old speaks up. "What story are you gonna read Granny?"

Tysheka glances at the book then speaks, "It is a very old tale, one that is supposed to teach a great lesson." She thinks about her statement for a few moments before she tosses the book aside. "I have a real story to tell you kids," the grandmother informs her grandchildren.

The many children waiting for her next sentence get excited.

"It's a lesson in life. An epic. And a tragedy. It may be unsuitable for children your age." The grandmother leans in close. "But it's something you must know."

The children's eyes grow wide.

"But we can get into a whole lot of trouble for talking about such things, so I will need a very serious promise that you will only keep it among your old grandma and each other."

"We promise!" The children answer in unison.

Old Tysheka smiles momentarily before putting that serious look back on her face. "Many of you have come to me asking why there are so few of us colored people, and so many whites."

Many of the children nod.

"There is a reason for that my little ones."

The children are not scared. Just serious sponges waiting.

The grandmother begins her story. "History books you find at school won't tell you, but a long time ago, there was a law..."

THE END

CPSIA information can be obtained
at www.ICGtesting.com
Printed in the USA
LVHW110027280223
740229LV00034B/544/J